Moving target

Steering with his right hand, Gadgets Schwarz grabbed the 10 mm automatic in his left and shoved it out his window at the other vehicle. As he fired, he saw the man framed in the open window drop his pistol and grab for his face, then heard him shriek at the sudden pain.

Guessing at the direction, Gadgets rapidly pumped two more rounds at the sound of the screaming man. He heard the high-pitched whine as one of the hot slugs ricocheted from the edge of the passenger's window, deep into man's left eye.

The driver, a man with an angry-looking scar slashed across his right cheek, raised his weapon and started shooting wildly at Gadgets.

The Able Team warrior tried to return the fire, then heard the ominous metallic click as the Colt's hammer hit metal. Gadgets knew there was no time to drop the clip and snap in a new one.

''Able Team will go anywhere, do anything, in order to complete their mission.''
—*West Coast Review of Books*

Mack Bolan's

ABLE TEAM®

ABLE TEAM.

Dueling Missiles

Dick Stivers

A GOLD EAGLE BOOK FROM
W❂RLDWIDE.

TORONTO • NEW YORK • LONDON • PARIS
AMSTERDAM • STOCKHOLM • HAMBURG
ATHENS • MILAN • TOKYO • SYDNEY

First edition November 1990

ISBN 0-373-61249-4

Special thanks and acknowledgment to
David North for his contribution to this work.

PROLOGUE

The heavy Antonov A-124 transport lumbered down the runway, then slowly picked up speed. Finally it exerted the effort needed to lift itself into the night sky over the vast plains of the Uzbek Republic.

Mikoyan, the stocky radio operator, finished giving his report to the base tower and turned to face the pilot. "Who was that strange man who handed you the fuel forms to sign?" he asked, thinking back to an incident he'd witnessed before takeoff.

"Another ground crew chief," Colonel Andrei Marakov Pushkomin replied, sounding bored. "A nobody."

"Just another unwashed Turk," the copilot observed as he kept his eyes on the numerous gauges and dials in front of him.

"He looked like the devil himself," the Ukrainian radio operator commented before the cockpit fell silent as the men concentrated on reaching their cruising altitude.

When they had risen above the thick clouds, Pushkomin opened the sealed orders. As he scanned them, he whistled. Their destination was the United States—a military air base in the southeastern part of the country. For a moment he wondered who the passengers he carried were, then he dismissed the thought. If it was important that he know, he would have been briefed.

He studied the instructions, then set the jet on a course toward the North Pole. Their flight path would take them over the Arctic Circle and across the Kara Sea where they would make coded contact with Soviet flight controllers stationed off Wrangel Island in the Arctic Ocean. Once they entered American airspace, they would be escorted by American jet fighters to the Air Force base near Texarkana. After the passengers and cargo were unloaded, perhaps somebody would explain the reason for this secret flight. Pushkomin shook his head. Probably not. Not if it was like all the others he had flown.

IN THE PASSENGER SECTION the twelve uniformed Russians again reviewed the schedule they would follow in order to confirm that the Americans were actually dismantling their midrange nuclear missiles. The sensitive equipment they would use wouldn't allow the Americans to cheat.

News that the two countries had agreed to advance the date when they would exchange teams of nuclear weapons experts had been carefully kept from both the press and the public. No announcement would be made until both teams had completed their first missions and were on their way home.

Their discussions were interrupted by an announcement over the speaker that the jet had reached its cruising altitude. Colonel Petrovsky checked his watch. "The Americans should be leaving in exactly four hours," he announced. The departures had been scheduled so that both teams would arrive at their destinations at approximately the same time.

"Timed like a ballet performance," Captain Natasha Comenskia, the most attractive member of the team, complained.

"We'll all dance with joy when this trip is over," one of the men commented, not bothering to hide his fatigue.

"But none as beautifully as you," Petrovsky said, smiling at Natasha, a former ballet student. The petite brunette, who managed to exude femininity despite the shapeless unisex uniform she wore, smiled back her gratitude at the flattery and leaned her head back to rest.

A serious-faced young scientist stared at him through his thick glasses and asked, "Will we see any cowboys, Comrade Colonel?"

Petrovsky smiled patiently. He had visited the United States before to participate in an international conference on nuclear waste. "Cowboys are in places like Arizona, not in the southeastern part of the country where we're going, Dr. Dolobin."

Dolobin looked disappointed. "What can we do when we get there?"

"For one thing, Dr. Dolobin," he began patiently, "you'll get a chance to taste some of the delicacies Americans enjoy." Petrovsky smiled to himself. He wouldn't mention the steaks and chops he had enjoyed during his last visit. Or the stores fully stocked with merchandise and few lines of shoppers waiting to buy items. He'd let Dolobin and the others discover these for themselves. Right now it was time to rest. He leaned his head back and closed his eyes.

COLONEL PUSHKOMIN STARED out into the black below him. They had been flying for several hours. He glanced at the small map on his lap and confirmed that they had entered the Arctic region. There were no lights visible below.

The burly black-haired man set the automatic pilot and ordered the other three flight officers to relax and have a cigarette before he turned and grinned at the anemic-looking radio operator. "Before you light that god-awful pipe of yours, Mikoyan, contact Nukus and inform them that everything is proceeding—"

But Pushkomin was stopped in midsentence as waves of flames raced through the interior of the aircraft.

TAMAR KARRIM SMILED as he thought of how easy this assignment had been. He was a heavyset man in his late thirties with the dark features of his Turkish ancestors and a wide scar that cut across the left edge of his mouth. Karrim was rumored to be an agent of the KGB, although none of the men who worked with him were certain of his employer. Some of those who reported to him suspected he was involved with the Iranians. It didn't matter. His deep, emotionless eyes and his humorless smile terrified them.

He had accepted the assignment several days before the base commander had received his orders from Moscow. It wasn't difficult to use the holiday time long due him and slip across the Iranian border to meet with the man in Meshed.

The job had sounded simple enough. A transport would be leaving the desert air base near Nukus within a week. He was to make sure it didn't reach its destination. Karrim wasn't told why. Nor did he care.

He liked working for Lubankov, even though the ex-KGB man's former superiors had issued a death warrant for him. Karrim was continually surprised at how American the Russian looked and sounded. Especially his accent. He sounded like one of the country and western singers featured on the shortwave radio programs.

Lubankov always provided the necessary materials. This time they were easy to transport and almost impossible for anyone but an explosives expert to identify.

Karrim's orders were to install woven sheets of a Czech plastic explosive as close as possible to the fuel tanks of the eight Antonov transport planes parked at the base. He was then to attach barometric timing triggers, set to go off when the aircraft had flown at its cruising altitude for six hours. After the plane with the twelve Russians had departed, the Turk was to remove the plastic explosives and triggers from the remaining aircraft.

It was one of the simpler missions Lubankov had given him. Of more importance to Karrim was the fact the former KGB man had also given him a good-faith retainer of one thousand Swiss francs. The balance of eight thousand Swiss francs was to be deposited in an account in Ankara when the job was successfully completed.

Security had been tight at the base and especially around the aircraft, but Karrim had had no problem completing his assignment. In fact, disposing of the unused plastic had been a simple matter. Without the triggers the material made an excellent and safe fuel. He had dropped the sheets into a barrel of burning waste near the base's garbage dump. The seven timing devices were buried in a barrel of thick waste sludge scheduled to be taken away before morning.

Now, as he drove his small gray Yugo into Nukus, he smiled at his success. Making sure he wasn't being followed, he wove his way through a confusing network of narrow streets until he reached a small concrete apartment house that looked as if it would collapse momentarily from old age.

There was nobody in sight except the wizened old man with the flowing gray mustache who always seemed to be sitting in the same place, semiconscious, his back against the wall, staring at an almost empty bottle of vodka.

Karrim walked around the back and unlocked a small metal door. Listening to make sure there was nobody there, he stepped inside and closed the door behind him before turning on a small, shaded ceiling light. He sat down at the wooden table and turned on a shortwave transceiver.

While it was warming up, he checked his watch for the time. Perfect. Only a minute to go before he was due to send the message. He counted the seconds as the hand moved slowly around the face of the clock. Fifteen, ten, five...

Karrim leaned forward and spoke into the small microphone. The message had been received in Ankara and would be forwarded to Lubankov.

The Turk turned off the set and leaned back in the chair, feeling relaxed and satisfied. He reached into his pocket and treated himself to a rare pleasure, one of the Turkish cigarettes he had smuggled across the border from Meshed.

As he inhaled the delicate perfume of the tobacco, he became preoccupied with thoughts of how he would spend his payment. He didn't hear the door behind him open until it was too late.

Spinning around in his chair, he saw the shadow of a man holding a 9 mm SOCIMI Type 821 submachine gun. Before he could grab the fully loaded 9 mm Glock automatic on the table beside him, the shadowy figure squeezed the trigger and sprayed Karrim with a continuous wave of lead until the walls of the small room were stained with blood and torn bits of body tissue.

Gingerly working his way past the widening pool of blood that now covered the floor, the elderly mustached man held the ugly assault rifle ready to fire as he leaned over and turned on the transmitter. He checked the setting on the dial, then squeezed the button on the microphone and gave his report in the soft Italian dialect spoken in the Lugano district of Switzerland. He listened for the brief acknowledgment, then turned to leave, knowing his message would be passed to his client.

The well-dressed Middle Easterner who had hired him didn't say why they had wanted the Turk killed. He really didn't care. The fee he had received for his few minutes of effort had been the largest he'd been paid since his retirement from the Italian intelligence service in order to free-lance.

1

The phone in Rich Levinson's bachelor apartment rang just as he was about to open the front door and walk out into the cool morning air. The balding, baby-faced man checked his appearance in the mirror next to the door. Halloran was a stickler for proper dress—he would check everything right down to the insignia on Rich's shoulders that identified him as a major in the United States Air Force.

Levinson glanced at the phone, but before deciding whether he should take the time to answer it, the ringing stopped.

He looked back at the mirror, once again examining his receding hairline. Outside of that he didn't look half bad for a thirty-seven-year-old former Vietnam Green Beret and jet jockey.

He pounded his stomach lightly. The exercise was helping. Despite Karen's insistence on cooking calorie-saturated dinners for him, he was getting rid of the thickness around his waist. If he kept resisting her fabulous desserts, he'd be back to 165 pounds, which was about right for his height of five-ten.

The phone started ringing again, and he was tempted to set the answering machine and let it take a message. But it might be Karen reminding him about the dinner-dance tonight. Maybe he could hint that something had come up. He'd been prohibited from telling anybody, even Karen who had top-level security clearance because of her position as secretary to the base commander, about the flight he was about to pilot. It was just like all the other special missions he had flown. Secret. His fortieth birthday suddenly seemed too close for comfort. All he wanted to do was marry Karen and start having kids. He lifted the phone to his ear.

The voice on the other end boomed loudly through the telephone. "Is this the bagel man?"

Rich recognized the voice immediately. Schwarz. Hermann Schwarz. Another bachelor like himself. They'd been friends even before Vietnam. Now they were just two war horses who still kept in touch when their duties permitted them to do so.

They hadn't seen each other in three years. Levinson wondered if Schwarz's hair had also begun to recede. It was the least one friend could do for another.

As he recalled, they were almost the same age, height and weight. They both had a deceptively mild appearance. The difference was that Levinson had seen what Schwarz could do in close combat. The meek exterior vanished to be replaced by a fast, effective human killing machine. There had been a great many times that he had been grateful Gadgets and he were on the same side.

He would have liked to spend time with Schwarz, but, as always, the "whiz kid" had given him no advance warning he would be calling.

"How's it going?" he asked.

As they caught up on current events, Levinson remembered how they had met.

They had both attended lectures at Cal Tech at the same time. Schwarz was the electronics genius who seemed to instinctively know the right answers to the most complex problems. Rich could remember the dean trying to convince Schwarz to accept a scholarship and go for a degree. Rich had worked on him, too, but just when he'd thought he had him convinced, Schwarz had dropped out and signed up for Vietnam.

His decision hadn't made any sense to Levinson. Why would anyone walk out on a potentially lucrative career? When he enlisted for Vietnam the day after graduation,

Levinson suddenly understood that people like Schwarz and he couldn't live with themselves, knowing so many of their friends were dying to protect their much-envied way of life.

When they met again, they were both members of a Military Intelligence Vietnam Special Operations Group—MIVSOG—out of Da Nang. Levinson remembered jockeying his Bell AH-1 Huey Cobra through countless deadly curtains of tracers as he ferried members of the Special Forces team into Laos and North Vietnam on one of their direct-action missions. He had made nineteen suicide runs for MIV before they rotated him back to the States. Now Schwarz and he were the only two of their SOG still living.

There was a difference in their lives now. He was still an air jockey flying top-security missions for the braided hats, while Schwarz had turned in his green beret. Gadgets had started a successful security consulting firm, headquartered in Minneapolis, with another Special Forces type: a Latin named Rosario Blancanales.

He wondered if Schwarz still recited the Special Forces prayer, based on the Twenty-third Psalm, that they used to shout at the VCs after one of their frequent bloody confrontations:

Yeah, though I walk through the valley
Of the shadow of death, I will
Fear no evil. For I am the
meanest mother in the valley!

Probably not, he decided. It wasn't the kind of thing successful businessmen did.

"I tried calling you a minute ago, but I must have dialed a wrong number," Gadgets replied. "How are you doing? Still seeing that gorgeous blonde?"

"Karen? Whenever they don't shove me into a plane and make me fly away."

"Tell you what. I found myself here in L.A. with a couple of days off, so I wandered down to Fairfax Street. I thought I'd pick up some of that god-awful food you New Yorkers drool over and take the scenic route through Palmdale and Lancaster.''

Rich's laugh was filled with sarcasm. The state highway that passed through the two towns before it finally reached the outskirts of the desert town of Rosamond, where he lived, was anything but scenic. There was nothing but the monotony of the high desert country and endless rows of retail shops stretching for a hundred miles on both sides of California 14.

''I've seen worse,'' Gadgets said in reply. ''The whole idea is that we can tilt a couple of drinks and get sick on some BLTs. You can invite the gorgeous one to join us if you're not afraid I'll steal her from you.''

Levinson was puzzled. ''BLTs?''

''Bagel, lax and ptomaine,'' Schwarz replied, breaking up with laughter over his joke.

''Lox,'' Levinson corrected him sternly. ''And you have to also have cream cheese, raw onion and sliced tomatoes. But not right now.''

Gadgets sounded disappointed. ''Got something better to do?''

''They got me scheduled out of here this morning.''

''Any place interesting?''

''Won't know till we're airborne. And if I did,'' Levinson added, ''I wouldn't tell you.''

''Guess I'll just have to see if I can locate Blancanales or Lyons and see what they're up to. Catch you next time,'' Schwarz replied.

Rich would have preferred a social evening to jockeying the huge Lockheed Hercules he was scheduled out on this morning. Especially if Schwarz brought his partner along.

He'd met Blancanales the last time Gadgets and he had been able to get together. Like Schwarz, there was something lean and mean about Blancanales. He looked a little taller, a little heavier and a whole lot slicker than Schwarz or himself. Which may have explained why Gadgets had kept referring to his partner as Politician or Pol for short.

Like Schwarz, Blancanales had a weird sense of humor, but one that Levinson felt comfortable being around. It was obvious that women were one of his pastimes. From what he remembered, they were as interested in him as he was in them. Every time one of them passed their table, they'd pause and smile openly at the handsome, conservatively dressed man, as if they were hoping he'd invite them to join the group.

Schwarz had once brought along a third man, obviously a close friend of both Blancanales and him. His name was—Levinson probed his memory for a moment, then remembered—Carl Lyons, although the other two kept calling him Ironman.

No one volunteered what Ironman did for a living, or an explanation of his nickname. Rich had assumed it was based on Lyons's build and personality. He was tall—well over six foot, and lean. Levinson had guessed he weighed under two hundred pounds. Even through his loose-fitting casual attire, Rich could see the outline of a powerful, well-developed body. He looked tough and dangerous, like an enraged bull in a bullfight, always ready to attack at the least provocation. Even when he smiled there was an emptiness in Lyons's eyes that made Levinson glad they were both on the same side.

"Say hello for me," the pilot said sincerely, setting aside his envy of Blancanales's thick, well-groomed head of hair.

"Will do," Gadgets said in farewell.

Rich Levinson left his apartment complex, jumped into his lovingly restored 1961 red Corvette and headed toward the Mojave Desert where the sun was making its first appearance in the eastern sky. In a few hours temperatures would soar, and the pilot hoped he'd be in the air before the July sun created dangerous waves of heat turbulence on the runways.

Levinson raced through the streets of Rosamond and onto Route 14 to get to the base before Brigadier General Michael Halloran peeled his skin off and used it to make a spare pair of the cowboy boots he loved to wear. It was a

fourteen-mile run from his apartment complex to the front
gates, and his superior didn't tolerate late arrivals, especially among men like Levinson who insisted on living off
base so that they could have some privacy between flights.

Halloran lived by the rule book.

Levinson finally saw the large sign that warned he had to
make a turn now if he wanted to find Edwards Air Force
Base.

"Next time maybe I'll just keep going straight," he
threatened out loud, knowing Halloran couldn't hear him.

He skidded to a stop as he reached the main guard post
outside the base, which sat on 128 square miles of the Mojave. While the MP went inside the small entrance structure to check his credentials, Rich glanced around him.
Over sixty-seven hundred civilian and military personnel
worked on the base. Landscape architects had tried to use
adobe-style buildings, wide asphalt roads, palm trees and
imported grass, but they'd had little success in transform-
ing the stark desert surroundings.

Finally the MP returned, handed back his identification
card and waved him through. Rich raced directly to where
the huge Lockheed Hercules transport was parked. He'd
get one of the ground crew to park his car later.

As he pulled to a halt on the grass strip along the runway, he was surprised to see the crew standing outside the
Lockheed C-130 Hercules transport he was scheduled to fly.
A base bus was parked nearby, with a load of waiting passengers.

He walked over to them. "What're you all doing out
here?"

His copilot, Joe Marino, nodded toward the cabin.
"Government safety inspectors inside, checking out the
plane. They insisted we wait out here until they made sure
it was safe."

Annoyed, Levinson climbed up the short flight of steps.
Three unsmiling men in business suits were running electronic wands along the ceiling and down the false panels.

One of them, who seemed to be the leader, turned to him. "Y'all the pilot?" he asked in a Southern accent.

Rich nodded. "Major Levinson. Who are you three?"

The one who had spoken held up the tag clipped to his jacket pocket. The man's picture was heat-sealed to a card that identified him as a special agent of the Defense Information Agency. Levinson didn't waste time reading the name on the card. He knew it wasn't the man's real name.

He had been exposed to a lot of government spooks, covert intelligence types, including those from the CIA, FBI, DIA and NSA since Vietnam. This man was a classic example. He looked taller than he probably was because of his thick, muscular upper torso. Levinson thought he was probably in his late forties, old for a spook. His hair was styled slightly longer than a crew cut, but definitely military. The man was probably from Air Force Intelligence.

Despite the conservative suit and tie the agent wore, there was something sinister and alien about him. For a moment the major wondered what it was about the man that made him feel that way. Then he realized it was his eyes. Except for the pockmarks and a strange dark ring around his neck, the man's face was normal enough. But his eyes were cold and glazed like those of a reptile.

Even that didn't bother the Air Force pilot as much as the sense of impending disaster that emanated from the agent. He had flown enough top-security missions since Vietnam to know when one didn't "smell" right. This one was starting to stink.

Karen had recently become interested in something she called New Age philosophy, which dealt with subliminal feelings and karma. Rich was always teasing her about it. Now he wondered if maybe there wasn't something to it.

He didn't have time to think about such things now, though. Halloran would come at him like a raging bull if he didn't get off the ground soon. He saw that the agent was still staring at him, daring him to challenge his authority. Levinson glanced at the other two. They looked like zombies. Three zombies checking out the Hercules.

One of the other men called out to his superior. "I need you over here."

The man nodded and turned to Levinson. "Y'all are going to have to wait outside until we finish going over this ship."

It wasn't a request. It was a thinly veiled order.

Levinson decided to let them earn whatever fee the Agency was paying them. He retreated down the steps to the fresh air outside.

A jeep raced up to the jet and stopped. The tall, erect, flint-faced senior officer who sat beside the driver jumped out and glared at Levinson. "What the hell's holding you up, Major? You're twenty minutes behind your scheduled departure."

"Spooks, General," the baby-faced man replied, then turned to stare at the three men who were leaving the jet and walking toward a dark blue car parked on the strip of grass.

Halloran glanced at them. "Our kind of spooks, Levinson?"

Levinson knew what the general meant. Halloran coordinated Air Force missions for the CIA.

"I'm not sure," Rich Levinson muttered, watching one of the men start the car. "You going to talk to them, General?"

"No, they're only doing their job," the general said. He watched them drive away, then took a deep breath and turned back to the pilot. "Load up your cargo and your passengers and get the hell out of here, Levinson." He glanced at his watch. "You're already twenty-five minutes behind schedule." He started to leave, then remembered something. He turned back and handed the pilot a sealed envelope. "Your flight plan. Open it after you reach cruising altitude."

Levinson snapped a salute and waited for the general to drive off before he turned to Marino. "Let's get a move on, Marino. You heard the old man. We're late!"

Twelve men and women in civilian clothes climbed aboard, while ground crews hustled large sealed crates into the cargo storage area of the Lockheed transport. Thirty minutes later, after Levinson and Marino had completed the usual preflight checks, the ground crew chief gave the all-clear. Levinson nodded to him and turned to his co-pilot. "Start her up, Joe." Listening carefully for any sounds of malfunction from the four huge jet engines, he put the microphone to his mouth and reported that they were ready to go. Then he glanced out his window. The general was sitting in his jeep, watching.

"You're cleared to take off on runway one," the military controller's voice said over the radio. Levinson turned away from the general and nodded at his copilot.

Marino picked up the microphone to the plane's intercom system. "Passengers are requested to fasten their seat belts," he said, then smiled at Levinson. "Just like on United Airlines."

"Keep practicing, Joe. You'll make a civilian pilot yet— if you ever get rid of that Brooklyn accent," Rich commented, trying to keep a straight face.

The copilot made a face and changed the subject. "Got any idea what our final destination is?"

Levinson tapped the sealed envelope the general had handed him. "Let you know as soon as we get upstairs." He concentrated on moving the huge transport down the wide runway and pulling its squat, heavy body up into the air.

What he didn't know was that one of three barometric timing devices was planted within a few feet of where he was sitting. It was armed and ready to start counting the four hours before it triggered the plastic explosives hidden throughout the aircraft.

2

The dark blue car exited Interstate 5 onto a quiet two-lane highway. The vehicle quickly pulled into a deserted gas station and stopped beside the telephone booth. The man waiting inside grabbed his briefcase and left the booth.

"I've got five thousand dollars for each of you," he said to the two men sitting in the front seat. Tapping the leather bag in his hand, he added, "We'll settle up just as soon as I make a call."

He walked back to the booth and closed the folding door while the other two remained in the car. Setting down the briefcase, he took out a small notebook and checked a number. Then he dialed 0 and a number in El Paso, Texas.

"May I help you?" an operator finally asked.

"This is a collect call from Thomas Hollings, ma'am," the man said, knowing the man on the other end would be waiting for his call. He waited, listening as the operator contacted the other party, and got permission to make the connection. The permission was given.

"Y'all patch me through," he said, exaggerating his accent, then waited as he heard a series of electronic beeps and buzzes. He was being connected to a telephone in Mexico through a scrambled message generator. "You should hear about it on the news tomorrow morning," he said, not bothering to use his accent or even to say hello. "The banker should be relieved."

The man on the other end grunted his acknowledgment. No pleasantries were exchanged. Hollings neither offered nor expected any. Theirs was simply a business relationship. He performed a professional service for which the client paid extremely well.

"One more thing," he added. "The banker did transfer funds to my business account, didn't he?"

The response was affirmative. Hollings looked pleased. He was getting closer to his goal. Soon he would have enough money to adopt the new identity he had already started to build.

He hung up and looked out of the phone booth at the men in the waiting car, then glanced at his watch. It would soon be time to fly back to Mexico City and to the delights that city offered. Hollings picked up his briefcase and loosened the silenced 9 mm automatic in his waistband, then walked to the rental car.

It was time to put the final touches on this assignment. He had a look of satisfaction on his pockmarked face as he leaned against the open window to address the driver.

The thick man behind the wheel looked up at him, and the man next to him leaned over to listen.

Hollings grinned easily. "Time to wrap this up," he said in a gentle voice as he eased the small black automatic into his hand and calmly pumped two shots into the right eye of the driver. As blood rushed out of the shattered eye socket, the second man pulled back and reached under his jacket for the revolver he wore in a snapaway shoulder holster. Hollings shook his head at the gesture as he pointed his weapon at the other man's carotid artery and fired, then pulled back quickly as a fountain of blood spurted onto the carpeted floor.

Moving as if in slow motion, he carefully opened the front left door and let the body of the driver fall out onto the blacktop. A sixth sense, developed from years of experience, told him that there was no life left in the still form.

Glancing around first to make sure he was still alone, he moved to the other side of the car and opened the passenger door. Then he carefully pulled the second body out of the car and let it roll onto the ground. This time he didn't bother checking for life. He knew that the man had been dead when he'd pumped the second bullet into him.

Closing the door, he quickly moved around to the driver's side, jumped in and shifted into drive. It would take him ninety minutes to reach Los Angeles International Airport, and his flight left for Mexico City in three hours, more than enough time to drive back to the city, stop for a light meal, abandon the car somewhere near Watts and hail a cab to get him to the airport.

All in all, a plan well executed—and a very profitable one. He glanced through his rearview mirror at the two bodies blocking the entrance to the gas station. They wouldn't be found until the morning attendant showed up for work at six.

He was glad he'd told Emile Wittsinger to import foreign talent. It would make identifying them more difficult.

ONCE THEY HAD REACHED thirty thousand feet, Rich Levinson turned the controls over to his copilot and opened the envelope. He studied the flight plans carefully, muttering under his breath as he did so.

"I just hope we've got enough juice in the tanks," he grumbled.

Marino stared at him. "So where are we going, Rich?"

"Over the Arctic," Levinson replied in disgust. "And then down to an air base in Russia near a city called Nukus."

"Why?" the copilot asked.

The major shook his head. "I wish I knew."

As Levinson and the rest of the crew concentrated on directing the huge aircraft across Canada and into the Arctic region, the twelve men and women seated in the rear cabin completed another review of their schedules, then put their plan books away.

Lieutenant General Arthur LaMans stretched and yawned. "Let's get some sleep while we can. We've got a couple of long—"

He stopped talking when he and the others heard a strange growling that seemed to come from behind the walls at both ends of the aircraft. The fiery explosion that tore through the huge transport sent all the passengers and crew to their final rest.

3

The secured telecommunications lines that connected the inner sanctums of the two capitals sizzled. Each side accused and threatened the other. Finally the American colonel, who was the security officer on duty, told his uniformed aide to call the President.

In Moscow an aide roused the Soviet president and notified him that both planes were missing. The Americans, he added, were accusing them of shooting down their transport and declaring they knew nothing about the Antonov.

In Washington key members of the cabinet and principal advisers were awakened and rushed by limousine to the Executive Office Building. They could be slipped in without any of the large, ever-present army of reporters, photographers and cameramen seeing them. Once inside the building, they were led through an underground passageway to the second floor of the White House, where the President waited for them in the Oval Office.

A similar group began to gather inside the Kremlin while Soviet citizens passing the forbidding-looking building went about their daily routines. None of them were aware that their country was edging closer to the brink of war.

"THE RUSSIANS HAVE BEEN known to destroy their own people to create dissension." The soft-spoken comment came from the gray-haired older man puffing on a charred briar pipe.

The President bristled. If it had been anyone else, he would have dismissed the comment without second thought. But not when it came from Horace Bigsby, who had been deputy director of the CIA for longer than the President could remember.

"But why?" the President asked.

"Could be smart public relations," Jim Harkins, his press secretary, suggested as one possibility. "If they get us to call off the treaty, we become the bad guys and they're the peace lovers to the rest of the world."

"It could have been a flaw in the aircraft," the President suggested.

"The plane was checked out carefully, sir," a senior member of the Joint Chiefs of Staff said stiffly, waving a sheaf of papers. "We had the preflight inspection reports faxed from Edwards."

"Then another country. A terrorist group. Anybody," the President persisted. "But how did they manage to get a bomb aboard the plane?"

"They couldn't, Mr. President," his security adviser argued. "General Halloran had a security team check out the plane."

The President knew Halloran. The man was a hard-nosed right-winger but a solid patriot. He'd never allow anyone to get through his people to plant some explosive on the plane.

A sudden thought worried the President. He gestured to the gray-haired Treasury Department official who headed the White House Secret Service. The man moved to the President's side and listened to the whispered question. "Remember '68?"

The Secret Service man nodded. That was the year Robert Kennedy and Martin Luther King had been assassinated.

"Make sure it doesn't happen again."

The stocky man understood. Congressional elections would be held this year. "I may need help from the other agencies," he whispered back.

"Use them."

The stocky man nodded and swiftly walked out of the office. He needed to wake up a few of his people and get the ball rolling.

A GRIM-FACED AIDE CAME into the austerely furnished room deep within the Kremlin and handed the Russian leader a hastily typed report, who then addressed the somber-faced men sitting around the table. "A group of our Eskimo comrades hunting on the Siberian tundra just radioed a report concerning two giant fireballs that exploded in the sky a few hours apart." The leader looked saddened as he continued to read aloud. "They reported finding scraps of metal over a thirty-mile radius." Shifting in his chair, the Soviet president finally said, "I must speak directly to the American president."

THE PRESIDENT REPEATED his conversation with the Russian leader to the group assembled in his office.

"A bad time to have to announce this publicly," the President's chief of staff, an astute politician, commented. "Especially with elections only a few months off."

The President nodded and turned back to the phone. He began to speak directly to his Russian counterpart, annoyed that they had to use interpreters. The Soviet leader asked if the President wanted him to release the report documenting the Eskimo sighting.

"No, not yet," he responded, glancing around the Oval Office. "The news about the missing planes is top secret until further notice," he said pointedly.

Slowly those present nodded.

"Do you have any thoughts about who could have committed such an insane act of violence?" the Russian asked.

The President repeated the question to the people seated in his office.

"Maybe we ought to look inside and not outside," a quiet voice said. The others turned to stare at him.

The President focused his attention on the man who was now chomping on the butt of a cigar. "Do you think we've got people in our country who could do something like this, Hal?"

"I think every country does, Mr. President."

Most of the men and women in the room weren't familiar with the man the President had called Hal. Some of them had seen him at meetings with the President before, but only in times of extreme crisis. Only a few even knew that his name was Hal Brognola.

Some of those present knew he had once been with the Federal Strike Force on Organized Crime. But few knew his current function. And even they knew only that he headed a crack counterterrorist group that operated out of its headquarters at Stony Man Farm, located in the shadows of Virginia's Blue Ridge Mountains. Only the President and a handful of trusted officials were aware that Brognola was actually the operations head of the hard-hitting group called Able Team.

Brognola's dire warning concerned both leaders. At his end, the Russian wondered if they should postpone implementation of the treaty until an investigation could be conducted. Recalling how much opposition he had faced in getting the pact approved, the President urged that there be no delay in proceeding.

The Russian leader again urged that they delay the implementation until they discovered what had actually happened to the aircraft.

The President finally agreed. He repeated the Russian's plan to his own group, then commented into the phone, "We'll dispatch another full team in a week. As soon as they arrive safely, you can dispatch your team." He looked around the room. "Anybody want to add anything?"

No one said anything. Finally Hal Brognola offered a suggestion. "If it were up to me, Mr. President, I'd play it close to the vest. Only the people in this room know what you're planning. I'd keep it that way and change the rules as you need to so that you're one step ahead of whoever's behind this."

The President nodded, then repeated the suggestion into the phone. This time he didn't need to wait for his interpreter to translate the Russian leader's agreement.

The President stood and dismissed the gathering in his office. "Stick around for a few minutes, Hal. There's something I'd like you to do for me."

Brognola nodded, and remained silent until only the President and he were left in the room. "It sounds as if you don't think our security was adequate, Hal," the man behind the large desk commented.

"My old grandmother used to say, 'Screw me once, shame on you. Screw me twice, shame on me.'"

The President laughed for the first time since he'd been awakened with the news of the sabotage of the jet aircraft. "Your grandmother, Hal?"

"What can I say, Mr. President? She wasn't just Italian. She was Sicilian."

"Are your men ready to go to work, Hal?"

Brognola thought about the three hell-raisers who made up Able Team—Carl Lyons, Rosario Blancanales and Hermann Schwarz.

Carl was in Los Angeles, calling in daily to see if the vacation he'd been forced to take so that he could recover from wounds incurred in a recent mission was finally over.

Blancanales had stopped in Minneapolis to help his sister, Toni, put together next year's business plans for the security consulting firm she ran for Schwarz and him. When Pol had called in yesterday, he had told Bear—Aaron Kurtzman—that he was leaving for Los Angeles to spend some time with his family. Brognola wondered how many extra pounds he'd gain from the continual fiesta the Blancanales family put on to celebrate his infrequent visits.

Schwarz had been spending the past month at Fort Bragg, North Carolina, learning another martial art to add to his survivor's kit. He'd called in and said he was also flying to Los Angeles.

John "Cowboy" Kissinger, Able Team's armorer, was on the coast, too, visiting the importer of a uniquely shaped carbon steel knife that supposedly cut through Kevlar body armor as if it were a loaf of bread. He was going to invite Schwarz and Blancanales to test the weapon since they were out there anyway.

There was one more thing Brognola knew. They would all drop everything and come running home at his call.

Home was Stony Man Farm. The family was Able Team. For Ironman, Gadgets and Pol—and for the backup staff of trained specialists at Stony Man—the family came first.

He smiled at the Chief Executive. "Always, Mr. President."

"We don't know who's responsible or how they did it, Hal," the tall, still-handsome man said, leaning back against his chair. "Do you think it might have been somebody who was in this office tonight?"

Brognola shrugged. "One thing's a given. Whoever's responsible isn't going to stop until the treaty's killed."

The President sat up and leaned across the desk. His eyes were suddenly hard as he snapped, "Use any resources you need, find out who they are and make sure they can't do it again."

"Ever?"

The President's voice had a steel ring as he replied. "Ever."

Hal reached into his inside jacket pocket and took out a leather case. He opened it and pulled out a fresh cigar. For a moment he gently rolled the tan-green cylinder between his fingers, watching it slowly turn as if it were a gyroscope.

"One more thing I didn't mention before," the man behind the desk added. "We're exchanging a representative from each team. The Soviets are sending someone over within the next twenty-four hours, a Major Tolstoy, to check out our plans and security arrangements. We'll be doing the same over there. I want that information kept at the need-to-know level."

"Someone from the KGB, Mr. President?"

He handed the Able Team operations chief a sealed manila enveloped stamped Top Secret. "Everything we know about her is in there," he said, then added, "They claim she's just a member of their nuclear observation team."

Brognola smiled cynically, stared at the cigar, then defiantly shoved it into his mouth. "You believe that, sir?"

The President didn't comment. He turned to the stack of urgent papers on his desk that pleaded for his immediate attention.

Brognola knew he'd been politely dismissed. He didn't mind. He knew the pressures the other man faced twenty-four hours a day.

"If we've got company coming, I guess I'd better find my boys and tell them to come back home so that we can start getting ready for them," he said, shoving the cigar case back into his inside jacket pocket.

The President looked up at him, then smiled gratefully before turning back to the papers on his desk.

4

Carl Lyons was trying to darken his already richly colored tan and read the front-page story in the *Los Angeles Times*. It wasn't often that the muscular blond man found time to indulge in the luxury. But he was under orders to rest and forget Able Team.

The top story in the paper was about the Nuclear Disarmament Treaty. As much as he was skeptical of the Russians' intentions, Lyons was pleased that they were going to take the first steps to get rid of their warehouses of nuclear bombs.

It was about time, he thought. The sooner the two sides start dismantling nuclear missiles, the sooner people could go to sleep without wondering if they would wake up the next morning. According to the story, almost a thousand U.S. missiles would be torn apart and crushed while the Russians watched over the next few years.

Lyons's first reaction was concern. Was this another fast one the Russians were trying to pull? The muscles in his taut, suntanned face twitched slightly as he thought about it.

No, he didn't think so. They were probably just as scared as the Americans that some kill-crazy psycho would set off a nuclear device when nobody was looking.

He remembered the late Peter Sellers in the movie *Dr. Strangelove*. That was fiction, but, as Lyons knew all too well, there were any number of psychopaths just waiting for the right moment to help bring the world closer to destruction.

The Ironman knew a lot about psychotics who killed for money, pleasure and/or causes they swore they believed in. It was his job to stop them. Not alone, he reminded himself, feeling gratitude for the two shit kickers who were his partners.

Carl Lyons wasn't ready to suggest that the elite group he was part of be eliminated. He knew the dismantling of the midrange missiles was only a first step. Wars would still be fought. Spies would still try to steal secrets. Drug dealers would still infest the sewers and try to drag the young down with them. And terrorists would still attempt to terrorize. There would always be a need for Able Team's skills as long as someone or some group could make money by keeping the rest of the world afraid.

How well he knew. He'd dealt with them all. From his time with the LAPD, where he had an enviable record for quick action and results, right through to today. It was that LAPD record that had attracted Hal Brognola, who was then with the Federal Strike Force on Organized Crime.

Lyons remembered their first meeting. How skillfully Hal had interrogated him, probing for his weak spots, his attitudes, his personal life.

Their subsequent meetings, at first seemingly accidental, were extensions of that first discussion. Lyons had begun to open up to the Federal agent's questions. And, in turn, the man from Washington had let him discover how he thought and felt.

Then had come Brognola's offer: if the bright young LA cop wanted it, there was a spot open for him with the Task Force. He had described the thankless job in honest, blunt terms. If Lyons joined the Force he could expect to live on the edge, constantly facing danger and death.

But before Brognola had let him decide, he'd warned him there were other conditions. The first was that he would suddenly cease to exist. Not merely relocate, but totally vanish. At least in the beginning. The second was that he couldn't expect to live a normal life again. No marriage. No house in the suburbs. No family.

Lyons had been married and divorced once. His son, Tommy, lived with his ex-wife, Jane, and the excellent choice she had made in the man who was her second husband. Without having to consider the offer too long, Lyons had signed on.

He must be bored, Lyons told himself, to waste time reflecting on his personal history. The big commando stretched and looked up at the cloudless sky. Not a sign of smog anywhere. Just the shimmering rays of the sun still climbing up from the east. It was a perfect summer day.

In the background Lyons could hear the sounds of bodies making explosive physical contact, and the groans and shouts that followed. Under other circumstances he would have investigated the noises, gun in hand. But here, sitting alone on a bench in the L.A. Stadium on a scorching summer day, he knew exactly what was making them. The L.A. Rams had begun spring training.

As a high school athlete, Lyons had been one of the stars of his football team. Then, like now, he had a burly frame that cried out for the pounding punishment of the sport. But an injury during one of the final games of his senior year had destroyed a promising career. His interest in football, however, had remained. Thanks to a high school teammate, Tony Palmetto, who was now a trainer for the Rams, Lyons was invited to attend practice sessions and any of the games he could make.

The trouble was he could only take advantage of the invitations when he was on leave from Able Team. And that only happened when he was forced to take time off to recover from a battle-inflicted injury. Torn leg muscles had put him on the bench at the edge of the field, too bored to care about the practice session or the stories in the newspaper.

He missed his two partners, Gadgets and Pol, even though they drove him crazy at times. It had been several weeks since Lyons had seen either one of them. He wondered what his two friends were doing.

Rosario Blancanales was either spending time in South Los Angeles with his huge family or charming another female conquest. Lyons had personally witnessed how weak-kneed women became when Pol poured on the charm.

Ironman wasn't jealous. Chasing women wasn't a high priority in his life. The few he'd been involved with had come after him, continuing to pursue him despite his best efforts not to get involved. Like Julie Harris, the FBI agent. He remembered her strong, handsome face and the strange emptiness he had felt when he had learned that a team of terrorists had cut her down at an airport. Had he fallen in love with her? He'd told her he had, but had he really meant it? Not that it mattered anymore, Lyons decided.

It would be a long time before he would permit himself to let some other woman really reach behind the thick wall he had erected to contain his emotions deep inside himself.

Gadgets, on the other hand, was probably nosing around the research lab of Cal Tech up in Pasadena. Schwarz was obsessed with keeping on top of the latest high-tech developments, especially in electronics.

As different as the three of them were, Lyons knew each had the ability to survive. The Team had taken on some of the lowest dregs of humanity, men and women who'd abandoned any right to be called human beings, and fought hard and tough until the scum had been sent back to whatever hell they'd come from.

Ironman was ready for action. He was ready to return to their headquarters at Stony Man Farm.

The ultrasecure complex, hidden in a secluded area of the mountains overlooking the Shenandoah Valley in Virginia, was only a short helicopter flight from the nation's capital. Perhaps Gadgets and Pol were back at the farm, testing some modifications that John "Cowboy" Kissinger had developed to improve their ability to survive. He had been raving about the new Colt 10 mm automatic built on the basic .45 Commander ACP frame. Kissinger claimed it had some very impressive performance statistics. Lyons had promised to join his two partners in testing the brand-new handgun at the Stony Man Farm range.

Lyons had a lot of respect for Cowboy. Not only was the ex-CIA and DEA weapons expert Able Team's private armorer, but in times of crisis he had the skills and strength to help out in the field. A terrorist staring at the six-two threat coming at him had to have a death wish not to turn and flee. With good reason. Cowboy left few survivors.

Lyons missed all of them.

Cowboy. Aaron "Bear" Kurtzman, the crippled computer expert who also functioned as an ad hoc assistant to Brognola. And, annoyed at having to make the admission to himself, he even missed Hal Brognola and his sometimes sour-faced comments.

As he thought of those with whom he'd shared so many near-death adventures, he became aware of a cylindrical object rushing toward him. Acting on instinct, Lyons twisted his body out of its path and whipped out the .357 Magnum Colt Python he wore inside his waistband under his thin tan golf jacket.

He spun around and watched the object hit the meshed wire fence behind him. Lyons stared at it as it wobbled around in the dirt; it wasn't a bomb or a knife, but a football.

"Shit, Carl," a familiar voice complained. "Don't you ever stop playing cop?"

Lyons lowered his gun and turned around. The tall bald man who stood near him had a shocked expression on his face.

"Habit," the Able Team commando replied casually. Tony was right. He was acting paranoid. Then he remembered Hal Brognola's pointed comment when the issue of paranoia had come up during one of their meetings.

"Even paranoids have enemies," the unsmiling man had reminded the team.

Lyons had lived a lot of years by remembering that everyone was a potential enemy, every place a possible killing field. He couldn't explain that to Tony Palmetto without telling him about Able Team. Which meant he couldn't explain.

Tony had been his friend since high school. The difference was that Tony had gone on to play football in college and then joined a professional team. Many injuries later, Tony had finally accepted a position as a trainer with the Rams.

"Want to throw a few with the boys?" Tony asked.

Lyons stood up. "Sure. Why not?"

"Because you're supposed to be recovering."

The Able Team warrior recognized the deep, sinister voice. He turned and looked at the speaker. Peter Costigan, stocky as always, stood sweating in his LAPD lieutenant's uniform.

Pete held out his hand to Tony, who beamed. The three of them—Carl, Tony and Pete—had been close friends in high school. Carl and Pete had joined the LAPD together.

"I forgot," Tony said, annoyed that he hadn't remembered Lyons's injury.

"It's practically healed," Lyons commented dryly. He was surprised that Pete knew about his leg. "You keeping tabs on me?"

Pete smiled broadly. "Some guy popped into headquarters, flashed his Justice Department badge and asked if anyone had seen you. When I asked why he was interested, he explained that you were under orders to rest. He practically ordered us not to let you volunteer to help us out."

"What did he look like?"

"Slick. Typical Latin politician type."

So Pol was in Los Angeles. Lyons started to get annoyed, then decided Blancanales was probably acting on orders from Brognola.

"Had another Fed with him," the police officer commented. "Nice-looking, college instructor type. Didn't say much. Just kept nodding every time the slick one opened his mouth."

Gadgets. He must be in town, too.

Hal was obviously determined that Lyons keep out of trouble. He smiled to himself at Pete's description of his two colleagues. If he knew what they were, what he was, he wondered if Lieutenant Costigan would sound so casual.

Lyons wasn't happy about their visit to the Los Angeles police. He knew Brognola was doing it for his own good, for the good of Able Team, but he was old enough to take care of himself.

He made a decision. "Got room in your car for a sight-seer?"

The police lieutenant hesitated before answering. "You gonna get in trouble doing this?"

Ironman donned a mask of innocence. "What trouble? I'm just going along for the ride."

Costigan shrugged, then turned and started walking toward his parked police vehicle.

Lyons threw a salute at Tony, then forced himself not to limp as he walked across the football field behind the policeman.

5

Lieutenant Costigan pointed out the changes in the neighborhoods as they drove through the city.

"Remember when you were just another police grunt, how they used to call L.A. a bunch of suburbs in search of a city?"

Lyons remembered. He smiled as he thought how frustrating it was to have to bite his tongue every time some tourist from Podunk and East Skunksville tried the line on him. "I remember."

"Not that way anymore," Pete said dryly as he turned a corner and headed slowly down Central Avenue. He pointed out the front windshield. "Now we're a city."

Lyons looked out. Central was at the heart of one of the toughest areas. Bars and liquor stores were lined up, one after the other. Lyons noticed there were few grocery stores and almost no shops selling other basic necessities. He'd covered the district when he was with the LAPD. "Some more bars and liquor stores, but it looks the same."

The police lieutenant shook his head. "You Feds are all alike. Can't see beyond your nose. Look at the people, Lyons," he snapped.

Ironman realized that there were no people on the street. The tough, unruly, predominantly black neighborhood he remembered had always been filled with wild excitement, sometimes too much for a cop trying to keep the peace. Now it felt like a ghost town. "Where are they?"

"Hiding." Costigan pointed out the shabby frame homes and massive public housing buildings. "Behind triple-locked doors and barred windows. They only come out when they have to." He pointed at some of the windows. "They know we're here. Somebody is always watching, making sure it's safe to come out."

"The gangs?"

"Don't you ever watch TV?" Pete was irritated. "Of course the gangs. This damn city isn't run by the politicians. It's run by the gangs. We've got 'em all. Black, Latin, Chinese, skinhead, Cambodian and Vietnamese. We even found a gang in the Beverly Hills area made up of rich kids willing to kill just for thrills. And every night each gang tries to wipe the others out and take over their territory." He looked frustrated. "They've got this town scared shitless." He pulled the car over to the curb and faced the blond man. "You know how old the average member is?"

"Young, from what I've read. Nineteen, twenty?"

"Try fourteen to sixteen."

Lyons masked his surprise. Although the Team had come up against the L.A. street gangs before, he hadn't paid close attention to the statistics of the gangs' membership. "How do they get away with it?"

"Bleeding heart lawmakers who write laws that let them walk away scot-free from just about everything."

"What about the people who live in their neighborhoods?"

"They've got what too many people want—guns, money, drugs. Now they're shooting for more territory to control."

"You mean out of town?"

"That, too. I mean, right here. We find at least one or two bodies a night down here. Sometimes rival gang members. Too often they're innocent kids who happened to be in the wrong place at the wrong time."

"Get rid of them."

Costigan held up a hand. "We can't. We do what we can. Arrest a couple of hundred of them carrying guns and drugs and haul their asses to jail. Next morning a bunch of sharp lawyers and some 'one hand washes the other' judges talk it over and decide they're still minors and need love and understanding rather than jail. The system sucks!''

Lyons was tempted to tell him how one sanctioned group—Able Team—had gotten around the red tape and game playing. But he knew he couldn't talk about the Team. Sooner or later he was sure that if things didn't change dramatically, Pete and all the other good cops who put their asses on the line daily would either quit or figure it out for themselves.

The lieutenant put the car in gear and pulled away from the curb. Lyons studied the empty street, then focused on the buildings.

He hadn't served in Vietnam, but his two partners had described the feeling of being in enemy territory. He had that feeling now. An enemy or a victim behind every door. He felt sorry for Pete Costigan and all the other good cops who were trying their best to play by the rules and do a good job. The trouble was that the gangs didn't bother with rules.

Costigan kept his eyes on the street ahead. "By the way, while you're in this car, you're riding shotgun."

They came to a red light and Costigan stopped. He pointed down at the space between their seats. Lyons had noticed the shotgun set in a floor mount when he'd gotten into the vehicle. A 12-gauge Mossberg fitted with a pistol grip to replace the usual walnut shoulder stock.

"That's only if there's an emergency. Otherwise you play sightseer," Costigan warned him. "I don't need any Federal heat coming down on me if you get yourself scratched."

Costigan finished his speech with a wink. Lyons smiled. "Anybody can trip and hurt themselves falling down. I may have to sue the city for not maintaining their sidewalks."

The lieutenant broke into a loud laugh. "You do that and I'll swear you attacked the sidewalk first."

Lyons held up his hands in mock surrender just as a dispatcher's voice broke the radio's silence.

"Officer in need of assistance," she announced, and gave the location.

Before the light turned green, Costigan swerved out into the intersection and pushed down on the gas pedal. Cutting in and out of traffic, he flicked on his flashing lights and siren. "It's a couple of streets from here," he yelled as he skillfully spun the wheel to get there quickly.

They turned into a narrow side street. A small crowd was gathered at the curb. Costigan raced his car until he was near them, then jammed on the brake. Drawing his police service revolver, he jumped out of the car. "Wait here. You're still an observer," he shouted.

Ironman grabbed the shotgun as he opened his door. Jacking a shell into the chamber, he held it ready to use as he moved behind the police lieutenant, his limp almost vanishing as he hastened to keep up.

The crowd opened and allowed the police officer to enter. The still-bleeding body belonged to a small black girl who looked four or five years old. Next to her was a tricycle. She had been pierced by a string of high-powered bullets. Her red-and-blue sunsuit was now stained dark red.

Ironman stared at the body and shook his head angrily. Then he saw the empty police car parked at the curb.

Costigan looked at the crowd. "Anyone see where the officer went?"

The frightened people shook their heads. Finally a nervous-looking gray-haired black man lifted his arm and pointed at a playground. The lieutenant nodded and walked toward it. In the distance the sounds of police sirens grew closer.

Lyons followed as Costigan spit out words of frustration. "How the hell could her parents have let her wear a red-and-blue sunsuit around here? This is War Lords territory. Everyone wears black and yellow here. Blue and red is for Kings of Hell neighborhoods!" he growled as he led the way into the enclosed playground.

Lyons paused and looked around. Much of the recreation equipment had been stolen or vandalized. Warnings to rival gangs that the War Lords ruled this park and the neighborhood were painted in Day-Glo colors across the face of the small storage building that sat in the corner of the concrete park. An abandoned dark blue car sat in the middle of the garbage-filled field, its tires and doors missing. Even from this distance he could see rows of holes in the fenders.

Costigan saw where Lyons's eyes were focused. He glanced at the car. "It's been used for target practice," he said casually.

The Able Team commando was surprised. "It looks as if it was this year's model."

Costigan didn't seem disturbed. "Probably was. Stolen and stripped. What's left isn't good for anything except helping gang members improve their shooting skills." He kept looking around. "Marlowe," Costigan called out. "Where the hell's that cop?"

Lyons cautiously moved behind the building as the lieutenant surveyed the area around the playground. "Back here," he called out as he looked down at the sticky red fluid spreading across the dirt. Then he turned as two police cars pulled up near the lieutenant's vehicle, parked across from the playground. Four uniformed officers jumped out, weapons drawn and ready to fire. One of them stayed with the body of the child while the other three ran toward the playground.

Lyons watched as another car pulled up behind them. Two men jumped out, both taking out .45 Colt Government automatics from their waist holsters as they moved quickly after the officers. Both wore tags clipped to their jackets that identified them as special agents for the Federal Task Force on Organized Crime.

Costigan put his hand on Lyons's shoulder and brought the commando's attention back to the two bodies: a black teenager still wearing a blue-and-red T-shirt and an officer in uniform who looked too young to vote. Someone had torn large holes in them with a high-powered assault weapon.

"Shit!" There was a coldness in the lieutenant's voice. Lyons understood. Rather than show emotion, Costigan needed to withdraw behind a private wall to mourn in silence. "I just went to his wedding a month ago. How'd he let himself get suckered?"

The newly arrived officers ran around the small building, then stopped when they saw the bodies.

Lyons kneeled and studied the dead men. "I don't think this kid was killed here. No blood on the ground." He looked at the abandoned buildings nearby. "Could have happened in one of those."

Costigan shook his head in disgust. "All this killing for control of a neighborhood where a third of the buildings are boarded up."

"I don't think so, Pete," Lyons interjected. "I think it's for money. Most time that's what crime is all about—money."

"What's the answer, Carl?"

Ironman couldn't tell him without talking about Able Team. "It'll come to you," he replied cryptically.

Costigan looked tired as he stood and walked toward his patrol car. "I guess I better call in and ask for backups," he said wearily.

Lyons watched him walk away, then saw the two men in plainclothes walking toward him. "How'd you two find me?"

The sandy-haired one in the zippered jacket and jeans shrugged. "Luck, I guess, Carl."

The other one, wearing a smartly tailored suit despite the heat, added, "And a police band radio that told us where one Lieutenant Costigan was going, Homes."

They had been calling each other "Homes" for the past two or three years. Some of the supposedly "cooler" street types had called one another the name for years as a way of identifying themselves as members of the same gang.

Lyons stood up and glanced at the boarded-up two-story tenements across the empty lot. "Pete could use a hand getting rid of some rats in those buildings."

Pol shook his head. "Hal's been in touch. He wants us back fast."

Ironman shook his head. "I guess we don't have time."

The sandy-haired man thought about it, then turned to Pol. "This shouldn't take much time." He looked at Lyons. "How long do you think, Homes?"

"Fifteen minutes maybe, if we put our minds to it," Lyons replied.

Pol weighed the comments. "Okay, *compadre*, but no more than an hour. The man's gonna have a plane waiting at the airport to take us home in two hours. And he'll kick our asses if we're not on it."

Nodding, Lyons led the way across the garbage-cluttered field. He glanced at his partners and saw them haul out their personal choices in handguns—Colt automatics.

As they worked their way across the field, Lyons pointed out the perforated car skeleton. Gadgets paused and glanced inside. "Hey, get this," he called out. Ironman and the Pol joined him and peered inside the front. Gadgets pointed to a series of minute dark spots on the floor. "Somebody did some bleeding in there," he commented.

"Way of life down here," Pol said in disgust.

Ironman was about to offer his comment when something caught his eye from inside the basement door of the building on the extreme right. Some kind of light.

Gadgets saw his suddenly alert expression. "What's up, Homes?"

"Pincer movement," the Able Team warrior said. "Against that building." His eyes focused on the boarded-up tenement where he thought he'd seen a light shining. Ironman signaled for Gadgets and Pol to spread out and cover him. "We'll have to find another way in," he said, resting Costigan's 12-gauge against his side.

As the three moved closer, they had the feeling they were being watched. The basement door was slightly ajar, issuing an invitation to walk in and investigate.

And maybe to die.

Lyons could see the glow of an incandescent light coming from the basement. He knew the building probably had had its electricity cut off. "Cover me," he called out as he plunged into the narrow alley next to the building and searched for another entrance.

Everything was boarded up.

He heard a whistle. It was from Blancanales. Lyons turned and shook his head. The only way in was through the open door. But there was another solution: get whoever was inside to come out.

For a split second Lyons regretted not having some of the equipment he normally carried when going into action. A couple of CS grenades would have dislodged whatever scum were hiding inside; they'd have surrendered, coughing and rubbing their eyes as they tried to wipe away the burning tear gas.

But he did have his Python and Costigan's weapon. And his two Able Team partners.

Lyons cautiously worked his way to one of the boarded basement windows. There was a narrow opening between two of the boards. He poked the muzzle of the short-barreled shotgun between the wooden slats and fired twice. He heard the rapid-fire chatter of the double O shot bouncing off the concrete block walls.

He pulled the trigger three more times, turning the shotgun at an angle to spray the shot over a broader area. Lyons then let the shotgun fall to the ground while he pulled out the .357 revolver and raced back to the door. The Python's six chambers were filled with copper-clad rounds designed to fragment on contact with what publicity-conscious manufacturers preferred to call "soft medium."

The Able Team warrior didn't waste time with euphemisms. To the ex-LAPD cop, they were 600-grain cartridges that hit fast and hard. They cut through bone and skin, tearing everything in their path as they cleaved through soft tissue.

Schwarz and Blancanales positioned themselves at opposite angles to the basement entrance, steadying their automatics with two-handed stances. Three armed teenagers, wildly spraying waves of burning lead from 36-round magazines in their silenced 9 mm TEC-9 automatics, exploded through the basement door and started racing across the cluttered empty lot.

Ironman recognized the stubby machine guns that street gangs had made their standard sniper weapon. He felt the burning slash of tiny chunks of concrete chopping a chunk of skin from his left cheek as they ricocheted off the concrete rubble.

He didn't waste time using the Python's sights. At the twenty yards that separated him from the teenagers, he knew the Colt revolver could end the life of a would-be killer.

One of the punks swung his machine gun at Ironman, unaware that Lyons's copper clads had torn open a cavity big enough to shove a large fist into the hole in his chest. The gang colors on his torn T-shirt rapidly disappeared as his blood soaked into the shattered garment.

"You're dead!" he shrieked, sounding more scared than heroic. He tried to pull the trigger once again, but his hand wouldn't obey his orders.

Lyons fired another round that burned its way into the drug-crazed punk's mouth. He spit out chunks of cartilage as he and his TEC-9 fell to the ground.

Lyons didn't waste time checking the fallen gang member. His instincts and experience told him the child killer was already helping shovel coal on the fires in hell.

Meanwhile, the other two hadn't stopped to see what had happened. They raced across the rubble-covered field, washing the area in front of them clean with showers of 9 mm lead.

Ironman turned and ran after them, realizing as he did that his leg no longer ached. But before he could catch up with the gang members he heard the whining screams behind him. The sounds were familiar melodies—the percussion of heavy metal hammers striking brass casings, then the echoed rush of fast-moving lead leaving muzzles, and finally the alto whine as the slugs chopped into still-living flesh.

Ironman knew the concerto well. Pol and Gadgets were the featured soloists. Their instruments were modified .45 ACP automatics made by Colt. The Government model.

It was the best music he could hear right now.

There was an expression of surprise permanently frozen on the second killer's face as he slid to the ground. Blood and viscera flowed into the rubble under him from three gaping wounds in his chest and stomach.

Turning his head, Lyons saw the third young hood stop and raise his hands over his head, still holding his weapon, then lower it quickly and try to empty its magazine into Pol and Gadgets.

Ironman jerked his Python at the punk and pulled the trigger.

But he was stunned to hear the hammer hitting only metal in the chamber. An unforgivable mistake. In the excitement of battle, he'd forgotten to reload. Mistakes like that meant death. He knew. He'd seen too many decent law-enforcement men and women die from it.

He flipped the cylinder open, dumped the empty casing and rammed a speedloader in, hoping he had the grace of the four seconds he knew it would take to reload.

The young punk had a sneer on his face as he lowered his weapon at Ironman and started to pull the TEC-9's trigger back. Suddenly Lyons saw the sun reflected on a sliver of metal thrown by Blancanales. The wedge-shaped blade of a knife sliced into the third killer's throat, opening a faucet of spurting red fluid from his jugular vein.

Staring in disbelief at Pol, the thug tried to hold the severed vein together. Unsuccessfully. Blood ran through his fingers and down under his T-shirt as he slumped to the ground.

Pol retrieved the carbon steel knife and wiped it clean on the dead hood's trousers, then joined Lyons and Gadgets. "Cowboy had us test it for him," he told Carl. "You ought to requisition yourself one." As he slid the knife back into the figure-eight rig strapped below the back of his neck, he looked at the three dead punks and the expensive imported weapons they had been using. "The drug business must be pretty good around here," he commented with an expression of disgust.

Neither of the other two answered. They had spent long hours talking about how dealing drugs was turning young men and women into crazed, power-hungry killers. The real enemies were the men who controlled the Latin American and Far Eastern plantations where the narcotic-bearing plants were grown and where the factories were located that converted the plants into the addictive poisons that were turning so many young people into violent criminals. Often the same men also controlled the rings that smuggled the narcotics into the United States.

They had all openly talked to Brognola about mounting expeditions out of the country to destroy the powerful men behind the world's drug epidemic. But he had turned down each request. The areas in which they were permitted to operate were limited to the United States. There were other groups working abroad to eliminate the sources.

"Not for them anymore," Gadgets finally replied to Pol's bitter observation. He turned and looked at the .357 Python in Ironman's hand. "Ever think of switching to an automatic?" he asked quietly.

Ironman glanced at his awesome-looking weapon, then at the sprawled victims. "Sometimes," he admitted.

"Too bad I wasn't carrying that new Colt Cowboy's working on. I would have liked to have given it a field test," Gadgets commented.

Ironman looked puzzled. "What new Colt?"

"A 10 mm. Named after their countersniper rifle. Delta Elite. We got to fire it on the range after you went on R and R. Kicks out .40-caliber rounds," Schwarz answered.

"Looked hot enough that even you might consider carrying it," Pol added.

Lyons didn't respond. He looked at the revolver he preferred to carry and shoved it back into his hip holster. "It isn't the weapon that usually screws up," he said. "Most times it's the person using it."

The other two didn't comment. They understood his reluctance to give up the familiar revolver. And the truth of his words.

They had all fought beside decent men and women who had made the fatal mistake of not reloading in time. None of them died mouthing noble statements. Usually their last words echoed the realization that they had screwed up.

The phrase *penny wise and body bag foolish* popped into Pol's mind. It was the favorite expression of the tough instructor at Fort Bragg who preached that the difference between a live soldier and a dead one was that the one who was still breathing hadn't worried about wasting the few cartridges that might still be in his clip before he reloaded.

"I'll check out that Colt when we get back to Stony Man," Lyons said, seeing the relief in the eyes of his two partners after he made the promise.

Three uniformed cops led by Pete Costigan, all gripping .38-caliber Smith and Wesson Police Specials, came running toward them from the playground. "What the hell do you three think you're doing?" Costigan yelled as he came closer to the three fighters, who were looking around to make sure there were no more gang roaches alive to take a shot at them.

"Helping out," Pol said, turning to him with a smile.

Costigan stopped and stared at the bodies. "Did you have to kill them?"

"I suppose we could have let them live to buy their way out of jail and go back to killing innocent kids," Gadgets said. He looked at Lyons and Pol. "If that's all the thanks we get, we should have just continued our vacation instead of being good neighbors."

Costigan looked at Ironman's cheek. "You shouldn't play with naughty boys who scratch your face," he said, mimicking a parent as he handed Lyons a clean handkerchief.

"I'll get a Band-Aid later, Daddy," Lyons said, then glanced at the bodies on the ground before turning to his two partners. "At least there are three rats nobody will have to worry about anymore."

"Four," Schwarz said, correcting him as he pointed at the roof of the two-story building. Draped over the edge was the body of a fourth teenager, an AK-47 with scope still clenched in his lifeless hand.

Costigan glared at Pol and Gadgets, then turned to Ironman. "These are the two who told me not to let you get involved."

Lyons nodded and muttered sourly, "I figured that out when you described them."

"Who the hell are you two?" the police lieutenant demanded.

"We're his baby-sitters," Blancanales said. "He's got to go home with us. But we'd like to come back and do this again sometime soon. L.A.'s sure a fun place to visit."

Pol winked at Schwarz and Lyons, then led them in the direction of their car while the Los Angeles police lieutenant muttered phrases under his breath he hadn't used since he'd left the Army.

6

Martin Johnson looked up from the stack of reports on his desk at the man who'd just wandered into his office. "How's the director feeling today, Mr. Bigsby?" he asked.

"Holding his own, Martin. I dropped in and had a short talk with him on my way to work." He lit his pipe. "Any word from your contacts as to who might be behind the crashes?"

"Nothing yet. We're still working on it."

"I expect you to find out, Martin," Bigsby said.

There was something about Horace Bigsby that made the reddish-blond man nervous. At first glance he seemed mild enough. And his voice sounded like that of an elderly professor past retirement who could never break the habit of lecturing.

His eyes were the giveaway. They were foxy. That was the description that most suited Bigsby. Nobody lasted at the Agency as long as Bigsby had without being shrewd.

Johnson wondered what the deputy director really wanted. As section chief of the Special Operations Desk, he was responsible for the special "wet" jobs. Among intelligence agencies "wet" meant killing. The word came from the vast quantities of sticky red blood that poured from bodies after a killing.

When the target was an important political, religious or business leader, the assignment went to one of the outside contract agents Johnson controlled. None of them knew who they worked for, and, if they did, couldn't prove it.

Johnson maintained discreet contact with defectors and heads of the various criminal combines, including the Jalisco Cartel run by Manuel Ruiz in Mexico. Johnson had made it possible for the Mexicans to slip their heroin, cocaine, crack and marijuana across the border in exchange for help in clandestine "hits."

Sometimes it worked the other way. For example, he had passed Hollings along to Ruiz with the understanding that he would be able to use the man and his resources whenever he needed them.

It was this practice that had gotten him involved in the current mess. A suddenly independent Latin American leader was making noises about seeking military help from the Cubans. He had to be stopped before he infected other leaders with the same idea.

Ruiz had introduced Johnson to Peter Mallincott, a banker, when he'd met with Hollings in Mexico City to discuss the problem. The three of them had made a logical case for keeping the Russians out of the United States.

Who knew where the crack in the door created by the disarmament treaty could lead? Perhaps even to the elimination of his job.

He had agreed to work with them, even introducing the banker to their Air Force liaison officer at Edwards Air Force Base, General Halloran.

Having worked with Hollings before, he knew the mission would be carried out efficiently. Now he had to respond to Bigsby's challenge. "We will."

The man seemed satisfied with the reply. "I know you will. I'd expect no less from the man who will move with me after the director is gone."

Before Johnson could voice his thanks, Bigsby turned and left.

He was wondering how he could get rid of Hollings, Mallincott and Ruiz when the phone rang. He glanced at the unit on his desk and realized that his private line was lit. He picked up the receiver. It was the banker, and he sounded frightened. "I'll call you back," Johnson said, and hung up. Setting his scrambler into operation, the CIA official dialed Mallincott's private number and waited for him to answer.

"What happened?" the banker added.

Johnson told him about the decision to keep the crashes secret and the revised plans, as passed along to him by Bigsby. They included the fact that a Russian major was being smuggled into the country to meet with key people in the Pentagon the next day to go over the new plans to ensure the safety of the Russian team.

"What should we do?"

Johnson tried to back off. "It's up to you," he said, coldly.

"You're involved, too," Mallincott reminded him.

Johnson knew the banker was right. He was involved, at least until he could do something about it. For the moment he had to cooperate. "Ask him to send Hollings back to finish the job properly. Sometimes the death of one person can be more effective than wiping out a planeload," he said.

As he replaced the receiver, Johnson began to think of the other contract agents he had on his string. He wondered which of them could take care of the three men.

PETER MALLINCOTT HUNG up the phone, then slammed a clenched fist on the highly polished desk in his antique-filled private office. The delicate Spode coffee cup jumped out of its saucer and crashed to the polished floor.

At least there was still hope of keeping the tension between the two superpowers alive.

He stared down at the front page of the *New York Times* that he had thrown onto the floor earlier. Not one word about what had happened. Not even a hint.

He knew he had to call Manuel Ruiz in Mexico and explain why nothing had been said publicly about the crashes. After all, there were billions of dollars at stake.

The Mexican might not express any anger, but Mallincott knew it would be there, hidden behind a mask of un-

derstanding and sympathy. The money at risk belonged to
Ruiz and the other drug syndicate heads who had backed
Mallincott when he'd started his own international bank-
ing network ten years ago.

For almost a decade Mallincott had pyramided the illegal funds entrusted to him into huge fortunes. The job had
seemed like second nature to him.

Mallincott's ancestors had been involved in banking for
hundreds of years. Until his grandfather immigrated to the
United States, where he changed his name, the family had
operated banks in the Middle Eastern countries of Bah-
rain, Yemen and Lebanon. Their customers were businessmen. Sometimes involved in legal businesses. At other
times, not so legal.

Those whose businesses were drugs, gold smuggling,
white slavery and money laundering had been acceptable as
depositors and borrowers to Mallincott's great-grandfather
and the men who had come before him.

It was only in this country that such ventures were un-
acceptable. He remembered being forced to resign from the
major New York bank he'd been with for more than
twenty-five years when they began suspecting him of laundering money for Martin Ruiz and his competitors, the
Medellín Syndicate and the Cali Cartel. He had then decided to go out on his own and had founded the International Bank of Commerce and Industry. Over the years it
had become a major financial institution with offices in
more than forty countries.

Unofficially Ruiz functioned as chairman of the board
of the bank while several of the other key investors acted as
board members. Naturally, because of their public stature,
their names never appeared on any bank documents.

The bank had begun as a small laundering operation, but
the profits his backers were earning from the sale of narcotics had quickly grown into billions. They had needed
places to invest the money.

"You can increase your income substantially—and legally—if the bank makes loans," he remembered advising the investors.

"To whom would you loan money?" Mayaguez, the representative from the Medellín group, had asked.

"Real estate developers, manufacturers of chemicals and plastics, the larger defense contractors and gun manufacturers around the world," Mallincott had replied.

Mallincott had started lending the laundered money. Ten million here, twenty million there, until he'd tapped into the international defense industry as one of their primary sources of expansion funds.

By now twenty billion dollars had been lent to defense contractors around the world. As mutual distrust between nations grew, so did the bank's business. Mallincott was always right there, ready to lend the defense industry more money to expand.

And now, thanks to a weak-willed President and a Communist leader ready to sell his country's soul for peace, the loans were in danger of being defaulted. It meant that Mallincott's own life was in danger.

He got up and moved toward the room's large window. Eight stories below the summer heat had raised tempers. Pedestrians were angrily scurrying up and down Connecticut Avenue while impatient vehicles honked at one another on the crowded street.

He couldn't delay anymore. He dialed the number in El Paso that connected him to the pleasant-faced man who lived just outside of Guadalajara.

As he had expected, Ruiz quietly pointed out that there had been no mention of the crash of the American transport—not even a rumor on any of the morning news shows or in the newspapers.

Peter Mallincott was so tense that he wasn't aware that the delicate porcelain cup, which had been one of his mother's prized possessions, had fallen and broken into a hundred pieces on contact with the hard maple floor.

He glanced at the frustrating newspaper headline again—
"American Inspection Team to Make Initial Visit to Russian Site Next Week."

The one thing he was positive about was that the newspaper headline was wrong. This wouldn't be the first visit to be organized. He'd financed the plan that had stopped the first American visit.

For a moment he wondered if the CIA official was lying about why the news hadn't been released. No, he would have gotten a call from Halloran in California if Ruiz's man hadn't shown up at the Air Force base.

"Something has to be done quickly," the man in Mexico commented in a soft voice. "The bank stands to lose a lot of money."

Mallincott agreed. He didn't want his bank to fail. That would make Manuel Ruiz and the other powerful men Ruiz had brought in as backers very unhappy.

And it would shorten his life.

Mallincott pointed out that he had already tried blocking passage of the treaty through the elected officials who owed him a favor. But there had been no way he could control the votes of every member of the Senate. Nor could his contacts in Russia gather support among enough members of the Soviet Politburo to stop the adoption of the treaty there.

He could imagine the short, stout, white-haired man who sat on the other end of the line calmly pondering if he was going to let him continue running the bank.

Or to live.

Behind the benevolent exterior of the kindly grandfather who took care of the residents of the village of Tala where he made his headquarters, was a powerful, unforgiving businessman. Mallincott had heard the rumors of what happened to associates who betrayed Ruiz or, even worse, failed.

He was determined not to fall into either category. He passed on the suggestion from the CIA official.

"Johnson sounded as if he was trying to back away from you," Mallincott warned.

"I'll have to do something about that," Ruiz said softly.

"I'm sending Hollings back to Washington. Give him any assistance he needs," the Mexican said.

Mallincott could feel his banking empire crumbling. All the years he had spent creating the image of a benevolent patriot would be wasted if the bank failed. The donations he had made to the right causes, supporting cooperative candidates for national office, even the gifts he had donated to the government, would all be useless gestures now.

Mallincott was so troubled that he didn't hear the stout, middle-aged woman who was his secretary open the door to his office and walk in.

"Is everything all right, Mr. Mallincott?" she asked. "I thought I heard a crash...." She stopped talking as she saw the hundreds of bits and pieces of fine china on the floor. Quickly she knelt down and began to push the pieces of the cup into a pile. Then she glanced up at the elegantly dressed man, who seemed oblivious to the loss of the piece of rare porcelain.

"What happened, Mr. Mallincott?" she asked again.

He stared at her, surprised at her presence, then followed her eyes to the bits of china on the floor. "I don't know, Mrs. Highland. Please leave it."

She left the room quickly while the banker returned to the more important issue on his mind. The only way to save his bank—and his neck—was to kill the treaty.

Even if it meant killing the President first.

It wouldn't make a difference, he decided. The vice president who replaced him would probably want to go ahead with the treaty, anyway.

No, he'd have to leave it up to Ruiz's man to use the CIA official's plan, or come up with one of his own.

One that worked this time.

7

The midsummer humidity of the Potomac basin hadn't penetrated the mountain country of Virginia where Stony Man Farm was located. Even the strong hot July sun didn't burn as cruelly in the quiet valley, not with the four-thousand-foot-high buffer that nearby Stony Man Mountain provided.

On most summer evenings the only sounds heard were those of birds whistling the latest gossip to one another. Or the crickets chattering. However, when the skies were free of thick moisture, those who were staying at the Farm could hear music coming from tiny hamlets like Nether and Fletcher tucked in the distant hills. The tinny sound of traditional songs like "Captain Jinks" and "Butterfly Swing" could be heard across the wide Shenandoah Valley. It wasn't difficult to envision couples dancing the Virginia Reel.

But it was rarely quiet inside the windowless, air-conditioned conference room at Stony Man Farm. Tonight the air was heated by the arguments flying back and forth among the four men who sat around the polished mahogany table.

Lyons was the most verbal. "Why can't the Air Force do its own baby-sitting?" he asked, looking at Gadgets and Pol for support. Both of them nodded in agreement.

Gadgets threw in his complaint. "Since when are you paying us to act as Scoutmasters for a bunch of Russian bears?"

"And bearlettes," Brognola commented.

Pol looked puzzled. "What's a 'bearlette?'"

"A female bear," Brognola explained with a small smile.

"And probably fat and ugly," Gadgets snapped back.

Brognola handed him an eight-by-ten photograph of the Russian team of observers who would be arriving in two days. The electronics whiz kid stared coldly at the group in the photograph.

"Like I said," Gadgets said sarcastically, "fat and ugly."

Brognola handed him a magnifying glass. "Like the one in the front row, third from the left?"

Gadgets scanned the photograph with the glass. She wasn't unattractive, even in the uniforms the Russians liked to wear. In fact, he had to admit to himself, she could be attractive if she'd do something with her hair and make-up—and that uniform. He handed the glass back to Brognola. "Who is she, Hal?"

"Dr. Irina Malkova Tolstoy."

"That's a real mouthful. Any relation to the writer?"

"Distant if any. She's a physicist. An honors graduate of the Moscow Technical Institute."

"And single?" Pol asked as he took the photograph from Gadgets and studied her.

Brognola nodded. "And single."

Carl Lyons glared at the Pol. "Zip up your fly, Homes," he growled. "We're not talking about your sex life."

"No, we're not," Brognola agreed. He retrieved the photograph and slid it into a manila folder. "What we're talking about is the most sensitive situation this country has faced since the end of Vietnam."

Ironman suddenly looked interested. Like Gadgets and Pol, he leaned forward to hear what the Able Team chief had to say.

Brognola took his time. First he reached into an inside pocket of a jacket and took out a leather cigar case. Opening it, he extracted a cigar and rolled it gingerly between two fingers.

Pol grinned as he watched Brognola go through his cigar ritual. "Cuban?"

The big Fed looked at him coldly but didn't reply. He waved the long cylinder of tobacco under his nose, inhaling as if he were sniffing a fine cognac.

The other three men in the room seemed hypnotized by the deliberately slow ballet. Brognola stared at the cigar as if he were examining a holy relic, then, without warning, suddenly shoved the cigar between his teeth and bit off the end. He leaned over and spat the bit of tobacco into a wastebasket under the conference table.

"*¡Dios!*" Blancanales groaned. "A thousand Cuban cigar makers just turned over in their graves!"

Brognola smiled at the comment. "Too bad that doesn't include Castro," he said quietly.

"Wishing won't make it so, boss man," Gadgets commented.

Brognola grinned at him over the top of the cigar. "While the Russians are here checking out that we really mean to scrap our Pershing missiles, a team of our scientists will be in Russia making sure they live up to their end of the bargain."

"Sounds like a job for Military Intelligence, or maybe the FBI," Pol commented.

"Usually it would be," Brognola agreed. "But not this time."

"Care to explain that?" Gadgets asked.

"No," the operations chief said bluntly.

He was aware, as they all were, that Brognola wasn't free with information it if wasn't necessary for the successful conclusion of a mission.

Lyons jumped in. "What's this got to do with us?"

Brognola studied the faces of the three men before him and decided they had a right to know everything that had led to this mission. "This is more than just a baby-sitting assignment," he said reluctantly. "Put the file on the screen, Bear," he called out.

"Coming up, boss," Bear's familiar voice replied over the conference room speakers.

Brognola gestured for Gadgets to turn down the lights. As he did, a pair of wooden panels parted and slid into the walls, revealing a large screen. Then a picture flashed onto the screen—a color photograph of a Lockheed Hercules military jet transport.

"This plane left Edwards Air Force Base thirty-six hours ago, en route to a military base near the city of Nukus in Russia," the chief said as he began the review.

He pushed a button on the control unit near his left hand. The picture changed. The plane was replaced with a group photograph of twelve men and women in uniform.

"The plane was carrying these twelve specialists," he continued, then clicked the button again to change the picture on the screen. "Twelve of the brightest nuclear talents in the United States."

Another click. A picture of three uniformed Air Force officers. The others could hear Gadgets suck in his breath as he recognized Rich Levinson standing in the middle.

"These three men flew the plane." He paused and turned to Gadgets. "I believe you were a friend of the pilot, Major Levinson."

The sandy-haired man became tense. "Were?"

"Sometime between takeoff and now the plane exploded over the Arctic."

"Russian sabotage?" Ironman asked.

Brognola shook his head. "We don't think so."

"How come none of this has been reported in the papers or on television?" Blancanales asked.

"Orders from on high," the Justice Fed replied.

The others understood. From the President himself.

Gadgets sounded bitter. "Why? Are they afraid people won't give a shit?"

"No, that people will. Even before they have the facts. We don't want the public running around taking shots at anybody with a foreign accent," Brognola replied.

"Why would somebody want to kill them?" Pol sounded puzzled. "What's in it for anybody?"

"We've got some suspicions but no facts. It could be a terrorist group or government who thinks they'd benefit by escalating tension between the United States and Russia."

"Like the Cubans," Lyons commented.

Brognola nodded. "Or political groups who see themselves losing power if our two countries make the treaty work."

Gadgets became quiet as he thought about the last statement.

"Put on the next picture," Brognola requested. A photograph of twelve men and women in Russian uniforms flashed onto the screen. "This is the team the Russians are sending here in the next few days." He turned to Gadgets. "One of them is the woman you saw in the photograph, Hermann."

Gadgets blushed as he studied the enlarged color image of the woman in the group. She had long, thick red hair and a narrow face. "I know," he mumbled.

"And you want us to keep an eye on them just in case somebody wants another crack at stopping the disarmament?" Lyons asked.

"No. The FBI will have agents protecting the whole team. You three will act as their escorts."

Ironman growled as he got up. "Count me out. I'm not the social type."

"And," Brognola continued, as if he hadn't heard Lyons, "you'll be armed to the teeth so that you can blow away anyone the FBI can't touch without the usual legal bullshit."

Pol raised an eyebrow. "You think it might be somebody high up?"

The Stony Man chief shook his head. "We don't know for sure. What we do know is that it isn't some local bunch of hopheads like the ones you three played stickball with yesterday in California."

The other three glanced at one another. Was there anything they did that Brognola didn't know about? The big Fed waited until they were facing him again.

But Pol couldn't contain his curiosity. "You got somebody watching us?"

Brognola smiled. It wasn't a secret he had to keep. "No, but some L.A. cop named Costigan called to complain to the Federal Task Force people that three of their men used an empty lot in his district for target practice." Lyons bristled as the chief added with a twinkle in his eye, "And to thank them for getting rid of some local scum." He pulled out another photograph from the manila folder and handed it to Ironman.

It was a photograph of the trash-covered field where Able Team had eliminated the four gang members. In the background Lyons recognized the cannibalized car they had looked over. He started to hand the picture back.

"Pass it around," Brognola said.

Pol glanced at the photograph and slid it over to Gadgets who stared at it with an expression of curiosity. He looked across the table. "What's the photo for?"

"Any of you look inside the car?"

"Yeah, I did," Ironman said.

"See anything unusual?"

Lyons thought back and remembered the stains. "There were a number of dark spots that looked like bloodstains."

Brognola nodded. "They were. The car was rented just outside Los Angeles International Airport by three men who used a stolen California driver's license and an American Express card. They used the car to enter Edwards Air Force Base, where they managed to get through extra security by flashing phony federal identification cards. They spent at least thirty to forty-five minutes alone inside the transport plane right before it departed. There's no direct evidence they were responsible for the crash, but I'd bet my life on it."

"So who the hell are the three creeps?" Pol chimed in.

"Were. A gas station attendant found two of them this morning. Shot to death."

Lyons looked exactly like the L.A. cop he had once been when he growled, "Got a make on the dead men?"

Brognola looked disgusted. "Couple of CIA types who supposedly got kicked out of the Agency and turned hit men for the Medellín Syndicate five years ago. We found their weapons on them. Nothing exotic about them. The kind of guns you can buy on any street corner."

"What about the third one?" Gadgets asked.

"The FBI traced him to the L.A. airport. One of the passenger agents remembered someone who looked like him catching a flight last night to Mexico City. Put the composite on the screen," Brognola called out. A close likeness of Hollings appeared. "Bear created that on his computer, based on the descriptions the FBI obtained from the guards at the front gate. I've run off copies for each of you."

The three men stared at the picture.

"Any of you recognize him?" Brognola asked.

"Looks foreign," Gadgets commented. "Could be KGB."

"Witnesses said he spoke with a Southern accent. His tickets were in the name of Thomas Hollings."

"CIA?" Ironman asked.

"Bear made a run through the whole network of government computers. Nobody in any federal file, including the CIA's, matches his description."

They all knew Kurtzman had devised ways of tapping into local, state and federal computers all over the country, even the ones with the tightest security.

Bear's voice boomed out from the speakers. "Like I said, I think I've seen that face before." The men in the room could hear him grinding his teeth in frustration. "I just wish I could remember where."

The computer genius's phenomenal memory was another legend round Stony Man Farm. If he said he'd seen the face before, they all knew he wasn't mistaken.

"Keep working on your memory," Brognola commented loudly. He turned to Lyons. "Anything else you want to say?"

"Yeah," Lyons said bitterly as he pushed his chair out from the table. He turned to the Stony Man chief. "Connecting with that car in L.A. seems to be too much of a coincidence. I think we're already involved. When do we start looking for him?"

"Not yet," Brognola replied briskly.

Showing his irritation, Lyons flopped down into his chair. "And what are we supposed to do? Just sit around and wait for his next move?"

"No. What you're all going to do is keep a close watch on the Soviet group and prevent Hollings or anyone else from getting to them."

Lyons looked as if something was bothering him. "How are we supposed to keep an eye on the Russians without them wondering who the hell we are or what we're doing there? First time they figure out how we spend our time, they'll hop on their plane and head back to Mother Russia, complaining about an American goon squad hanging all over them."

Blancanales and Schwarz muttered their agreement.

Brognola looked at their annoyed faces. "You'll leave for Edwards Air Force Base within twenty-four hours." The chief looked at the irritated expressions on their faces and added, "Dressed as commissioned officers."

"My mother never raised me to be a baby-sitter for a bunch of Russians," Blancanales grumbled.

"Carl and you will be captains," Brognola replied, then turned to Gadgets. "Since you're probably the one of the three who has any real knowledge about nuclear technology, you'll head the team as a major."

"Does that mean I've got to wear a uniform all the time?" Gadgets asked, looking disgusted.

"Most of the time. Any complaints?"

"Have you been in Washington during the summer?" Gadgets asked.

"You've been in hotter places," the operations chief reminded him.

"But I didn't have to worry about my clothes killing me as well," Gadgets snapped.

Brognola became silent as he studied the three men sitting around the table. "Okay," he announced. "You wear uniforms when you first meet the Russian major." He looked at Lyons. "That means you, too, Carl."

Ironman nodded.

Brognola turned to Gadgets. "After you get done with the briefing and drive her to the safehouse, you can resume wearing street clothes." He glared at each of the three in turn as he added, "Neat, tasteful clothes. Not the kind of things I've sometimes seen you wear."

Pol looked hurt. "And to think I spend a small fortune on my wardrobe."

The Stony Man chief nodded. "You do, but these other two slobs do their shopping at the Salvation Army."

"Enough about our clothes," Ironman said. "I've got one simple question—how the hell are we supposed to get into nuclear shop talk with the Russians?" He glanced at Gadgets, then turned back to Brognola. "Not all of us keep up with what's going on in science like the boy wonder across the table."

"For one thing, you won't be expected to discuss such sensitive subjects as the status of our nuclear research," Brognola said. Both Ironman and Pol exhaled in relief. "However, you'll have to memorize some buzz words commonly thrown around by professionals in the field. Bear's got a class arranged for you tonight. And you're all required to attend. Especially you, Hermann," he added, staring at the electronics whiz.

Gadgets looked surprised. "How come?"

"You're meeting Major General Cassidy, who's coordinating our end of implementing the arms treaty, and the Russian major at the Pentagon in the morning." He grinned at Gadget's surprised expression. "The major's arriving ahead of the rest of the group to go over our plans for dismantling the Pershing missiles. And the plans for keeping her group alive so that they're able to watch us do it.''

Lyons gave Gadgets a sympathetic look. "You can come back after it's over and tell us what a charmer she turned out to be.''

"You two will find that out for yourselves," Brognola snapped at Lyons and Blancanales. "She's due in on the 10:00 a.m. flight from London at Dulles tomorrow. You're meeting her there and making sure she gets to the Pentagon alive.''

Blancanales made a face at Gadgets. "How come we get stuck with the dirty work? She probably doesn't even speak English," Ironman muttered.

"Actually, her English is acceptable," the big Fed said.

"Why not let Pol play Sir Galahad all the way? He already speaks two languages," Schwarz said, showing his dislike at having to act as the escort to a Russian.

"Three," Blancanales said, preening. "What about the language of love?'' He turned to Gadgets and winked. "Look at the bright side," he said mockingly. "Maybe the Russian major will give you some lessons in that department.'' Pol looked at the impatient stare Brognola was giving him and threw up his hands in surrender.

Lyons suddenly looked concerned. "You know how paranoid the Russians are. If we just walk up and say, 'Hi, we're from the American Government, let's go for a drive,' she'll probably start screaming for the cops or the KGB.''

"We had our embassy in Moscow give her photographs of the three of you.''

"And she's still coming?'' Pol grinned at Gadgets. "They must be on the level about wanting this treaty to go through.''

"Great," Lyons grumbled loudly. "Now the KGB has some first-class pictures of us to pass out to terrorists.''

"Of two captains and a major? I figure they're like our intelligence people. Give them something free and they'll decide it isn't worth having. Except to help Major Tolstoy identify her welcoming committee," the Stony Man operations chief said as he stood up. He looked at them, waiting for their reaction.

"I guess it makes sense," Lyons admitted.

Pol nodded in agreement, then glanced at Gadgets. "We don't have to wear mustaches or beards or anything like that, do we?"

"If I thought they'd improve your looks, yes," Brognola said blandly. "But after thinking about it, no, you don't. Just body armor." Brognola turned and walked out of the conference room.

"Was he saying something nice or insulting us?" Pol asked, feigning innocence.

"I think what he was saying is that the meeting is over," Bear's voice called from the loudspeakers. "Class begins at seven tonight. Meantime, *dos ridanya* to all of you."

"Thanks," Gadgets said disgustedly.

Lyons stared at the sour expression on Schwarz's face. "What the hell did Bear say?"

"That was Russian for 'Have a nice day,' gentlemen," Bear called out. "Don't forget to bring pads and lots of sharpened pencils. But you can skip apples for the teacher. Knowing you three, they'd probably be poisoned."

8

It wasn't quite 5:00 a.m. and all the houses that rimmed Lake Barcroft in the upper-middle-class town of Sleepy Hollow were still dark. The majority of residents along Maryknoll Lane worked in senior government positions, or for corporations whose existence depended on government contracts.

The small panel van traveling along the two-lane road moved slowly while the uniformed driver studied the numbers on the houses they passed. The man sitting next to him also wore the messenger service's uniform.

The uniforms, like the van, were stolen. The men to whom the uniforms belonged were dead, killed last night as they were pulling into the messenger service garage. Their bodies had been dropped into the Potomac River.

The man next to the driver kept looking at a piece of paper in his left hand. "We're looking for 11250," he said for the third time since they'd turned onto the quiet country road.

The painted sign on each side of the van announced that it was the property of a messenger service. Anyone noticing it would assume that one of their neighbors was receiving some important document that couldn't wait to be handled by the regular mail. If they bothered studying the three men in the van, they would see unimpressive blue-collar types similar to those who fixed their plumbing and electricity, delivered groceries or appliances, or carried away the garbage.

Had they been able to see inside the van they would have jumped to different conclusions. The man seated next to the driver fondled a Smith & Wesson Model 59, fitted with a sound suppressor. On the floor next to the driver was a silenced 9 mm Uzi automatic pistol, loaded with hollow-point cartridges.

Behind them a third uniformed man sat on a folding jump seat, cleaning a huge .357 Magnum Desert Eagle automatic, fitted with a long sound suppressor. He kept staring out the side windows at the still lake, as he pushed the cloth-tipped swab in and out of the six-inch barrel. "It's so damn quiet around here," he complained.

"Be noisy enough in a little while," the man next to the driver replied.

The driver turned the wheel slightly as Maryknoll Lane curved around the lake. There was a two-story wooden structure on the rim of the cul-de-sac ahead. The two men in the van could see the black wrought-iron numbers nailed to the white wooden mailbox post. It was the address they wanted. They could read the name painted on the old-fashioned mailbox—Martin Johnson.

Their orders had been simple. Collect the papers the man handed them and then eliminate him. They didn't know why. All that mattered was that they were getting paid for doing it.

"Keep the engine running," the other man told the driver as he opened his door and got out, partially hiding the hand holding the Smith & Wesson under his opened jacket. He started walking toward the front door when it opened. The third man slid the side door open and eased his way out, scanning the area as he gripped the .357 in his right hand.

The reddish-blond man who stood in the doorway was still in his pajamas and robe. He signaled for the man to come closer. "I've got it right in here," he whispered.

A woman's voice called out from inside the house. "Who's at the door, Martin?"

"Nobody, dear. Just a messenger from the office with an envelope," he replied loudly. He turned and reached down.

When he turned back to the uniformed man, he was holding a slim leather briefcase.

"Tell Hollings I need these back as soon as he makes copies," he whispered nervously.

"I don't think you're gonna need these back," the uniformed man replied as he fired three rounds into Johnson's stomach.

As the CIA official fell, the man in the messenger service uniform reached down and started to pick up the attaché case when the plain-faced woman came to the door, still tying her long robe.

"Martin," she called out, "are you coming back to...?"

She saw the body on the ground, then stared at the man holding the automatic pistol and began to scream hysterically. The thug leaning against the van swung his huge Israeli-made handgun in the direction of her chest and jerked off two rounds. The massive .357 Magnum slugs exploded into her chest, tearing away skin, flesh and blood vessels. Unaware she was dying, the woman screamed until the blood from her ruptured vessels gagged her. She was still twitching as she hit the ground.

The gunmen raced back to the van and headed down Maryknoll Lane and onto Sleepy Hollow Road.

"What time is it?" the driver asked.

The other man sitting up front checked his watch. "Five-fifteen."

"Good. We're supposed to meet Wittsinger and the client back at the motel at 5:45 a.m."

He checked in the rearview mirror. The road was empty. They were the only vehicle in sight. A piece of cake, he thought as he slowed the van down. No point getting a ticket now. Especially since they were being paid for each killing. And the German had promised that they would have somebody else to terminate today.

EVEN WITH SEVEN HOURS of sleep Hollings was still exhausted. Dragging himself out of the motel bed, he glanced out the window. It was morning. A typical hot, sticky

summer morning in Washington, D.C. Wittsinger should
be arriving with the men he had lined up at any moment.

As he dragged himself into the bathroom and turned on
the shower, he reviewed the morning schedule. Three of the
men Wittsinger had recruited were picking up the documents from Johnson at his home, then coming back here.
He'd send them to the airport to kill the Russian officer and
plant the classified report on her body *if* she made it impossible for them to bring her to this room.

If they did have to kill her, Hollings prayed that the police showed up before the men got away. A shoot-out killing all of them would save him the trouble of having to do
it himself later.

It had been an exhausting twenty-four hours, he thought
as he stepped under the stinging bite of the hot shower. He
had been on the move constantly since the mission had begun. The Air Force base, Mexico City, then back to Washington yesterday to have lunch with Johnson and to salvage
the mission.

He thought about the recruiter he'd hired to find him
local talent. After Ruiz ordered him back to the United
States, Hollings had planned to use Shiite terrorists, but the
fee quoted to him sounded too high. And he wasn't certain
they wouldn't also be working for somebody else at the
same time. So he'd contacted Wittsinger.

He felt badly about Ruiz's orders concerning Johnson.
Probably something to do with a favor the CIA official had
refused to do for him.

Nobody said no to Ruiz, not if you wanted to continue
living. The head of the Jalisco Syndicate was one of the
most powerful drug distributors in the Western Hemi-
sphere. More than a dozen U.S. agents had vanished in
Mexico trying to kidnap him across the border. Hollings
had been paid for making them disappear. Permanently.

He owed Johnson for helping him escape to the United
States. It had been Martin Johnson, then chief of station in
Turkey, who had traded him a new identity for KGB se-
crets, and introduced him to his first non-Russian client, the

head of a Lebanese drug syndicate who needed a pushy competitor, with high government connections, eliminated. If there had been any way to save Johnson, Hollings would have. But in this dog-eat-dog-world there simply wasn't.

Hollings looked around the dully furnished room. Never trust a German to find someplace to stay that was pleasing. Wittsinger had selected the small truckers' motel on Route 301 just over the Maryland state line as their headquarters. It was depressingly familiar. The same prints he had seen in a hundred similar motels were hanging on the walls, doing a poor job of hiding the concrete block walls. The only worthwhile touches in the cookie-cutter box was the king-size bed and the hot shower in the bathroom.

He checked his watch. It was time to call the banker and make him feel secure. Ruiz's orders.

"I hope Ruiz realizes I can't control the President," Mallincott whined when he got on the line.

"Y'all know he realizes that," Hollings replied in his most comforting plantation accent. "That's why he sent me back. You're too valuable an asset to him to waste on this."

As he hung up, he smiled, remembering the Mexican's last words. *Like Johnson, the banker has become a liability.*

Hollings didn't waste time wondering who would take Mallincott's place at the bank. That wasn't his department. Ruiz's orders would have to wait until he no longer needed the banker.

And he had more pleasant things to think about.

As he waited for Wittsinger and his men to arrive, he studied the picture of the female Russian officer Johnson had left for him at the motel. He knew her well. Too well, he recalled bitterly. Much too well. She was a woman from his past, from the time he'd spent at the school in Gorky. The redhead had spurned him then, but she wouldn't do so again.

She was unfinished business, Hollings thought. For fifteen years he'd wondered if he'd ever have the opportunity of completing what he'd started to do back at the training school. Now that moment was almost at hand. But he would have to make sure Ruiz didn't hear about her. The Mexican was puritanical about mixing business with pleasure.

He owed Irina Tolstoy. She had reported him, had mistaken his advances for something more. And he intended to repay her for every moment of the fear he had lived through, hiding from the KGB, fearing that every knock at the door was one of their men.

Johnson's idea was excellent. She would be found with classified American documents on her and the body of her American military escort nearby.

Sitting on the bed with his head resting against the wall, Hollings put down the photograph and concentrated his thoughts on reviewing every detail of the mission. Three of the men Wittsinger had hired were supposed to steal a messenger service van before they went to pick up the documents. He assumed they had done so and were on their way back.

He walked into the bedroom and opened his suitcase. As he put on the pair of lightweight khaki slacks and a short-sleeved powder blue shirt he had packed, he heard a knock on the door. He reached under his pillow for the silenced 9 mm Beretta 92 SB Compact automatic, loaded with hollowpoints. Moving slowly to the door, he called out "Who is it?" in a perfect Southern drawl.

"They're back," the harsh, German-accented voice replied.

Kicking off the safety of the powerful weapon he held in his left hand, Hollings opened the door and moved back quickly. Wittsinger stood in the corridor, carrying an attaché case. Hollings lowered the gun and turned away. He hated looking at the German's scarred face.

Wittsinger handed him the attaché case. Hollings looked at the handle. It was covered with dried blood.

"What's that from?" he asked, staring at the blood as the German walked into the motel room and kicked the door shut.

"You said you wanted it to look as if he was killed during a robbery," Wittsinger reminded him.

"Any trouble?"

"They said some woman came running out of his house and started screaming. They had to kill her," the German replied. "But at least they got away before anybody else showed up."

That wasn't part of their orders. The quality of hired help was getting worse.

"Where are your men?" Hollings asked.

"Waiting outside near the pool. You said you wanted my men to pick up someone at Dulles?"

Hollings retrieved the photograph from the bed and handed it to the stocky man. "Send three of them to get her."

"Looks like a Russian officer," Wittsinger commented, studying it.

"She is. She may or may not be in her uniform when she arrives on the flight from London this morning. But they can't miss the red hair. Glows like a damn neon sign."

Wittsinger nodded but made no comment. He looked down at the leather case sitting on the floor near him. "Is she the one they're supposed to plant some of the papers on after they—"

"Yes, but not yet," Hollings said, interrupting him.

Wittsinger looked confused. "I thought they were supposed to—"

"Later. There's been a slight change in the plan. Have them bring her here."

The German's face hardened. "And if she refuses to come?"

Hollings forced the attaché open with a pocketknife. Thumbing through the folder of documents inside, he se-

lected a memorandum stamped Confidential. He handed
it to the West German. ''If they're forced to leave her, make
sure they plant this on her body.''

9

The seductively dressed redhead sat alone and dozed as the half-empty Eastern shuttle flight climbed above La Guardia Airport and droned its way toward Washington. She sensed the glances of interest from the handful of male passengers aboard. It always happened, although few of them ever actually got the courage to approach her.

Irina Malkova Tolstoy knew she was attractive, even pretty, when she found that useful. She had worked hard at being beautiful. At thirty-two she looked as good, if not better, than she had at twenty.

But at this moment she didn't care what she looked like. That could wait until she would be required to put on the uniform that identified her as a major in the Soviet army. Then she would need makeup to counteract the sexless qualities of the loose-fitting, olive-toned costume the Soviet leaders insisted she wear.

She had been flying for almost sixteen hours. The form-fitting Levi's she'd worn since she'd started the journey were cutting into her, the thin cotton western-style shirt was acquiring the odor of her perspiration, and she was starting to feel fatigue dueling with that part of her that warned her to stay awake and alert.

The fatigue was starting to win.

What she needed was a bath, some sleep and fresh clothes. But a bath and sleep wouldn't be available for hours. She would have to stop in a bathroom when they landed and put on a more feminine dress.

She sat up quickly and forced herself to stare out of the window at the cloudless world outside. Twenty thousand feet below, the monotonous view of city evolved into sprawling suburbs, which in turn became farms and wooded areas until another city replaced them.

There was too much to finish before she could allow herself to rest. She forced herself to go over her last interview with Comrade Colonel Sheveresky.

"The orders are explicit," the stocky bearded man had growled. "Your first responsibility is to make sure the Americans are sincere. Your second is to assure the safety of our people."

She remembered the pleased expression on his face when she had interrupted him. "And my third is to keep my eyes and ears open for any useful information the Americans haven't locked up in their safes," she had replied briskly.

"Exactly," the powerful-looking man who was her case officer in Directorate Nine of the Committee for State Security had said.

Directorate Nine was the special group the Executive Committee of the KGB had quickly organized when the new arms reduction treaty had been signed. The committee's mandate was to prevent defections and to take advantage of any information about American arms development that might become available. The majority of its agents were among the elite of the more than half million people the KGB employed around the world—engineers, chemists and physicists like herself.

"Any information you can gather about the disappearance of our comrades will be helpful," he'd added.

She'd been briefed on the missing Antonov transport. She had known some of the nuclear specialists who had vanished on that first, secret mission. But none had been close enough for her to mourn them.

Sheveresky had stood up and come out from behind his desk so that he was close to her when he offered her advice. "The state will deal with Lubankov appropriately when he's located. Not you, no matter what he's done. Is that understood, Irina Malkova?''

She had lowered her eyes and muttered, "Understood."

Both she and her superior knew she couldn't abandon her search. Not for Lubankov. Even the mention of his name—something she prohibited herself from saying—made the fury she felt in the deepest part of her soul erupt. The man had tried to rape her—he had violated a friendship.

He had cost her more than he would ever know. Even after the psychiatrists had spent months counseling her she could never again share more than momentary lust with any man, not even with the senior lieutenant she had been engaged to before she'd joined the recruits in Lubankov's sabotage training class.

Now she was only good for serving her country in whatever task they assigned her. Once she had been a promising young engineer. The KGB training had been an afterthought by her superiors, protection against a time when the combination of scientific skills and intelligence training might prove useful.

The intelligence service had been a godsend. Each man against whom they'd pitted her was a substitute for Lubankov. Someone to seduce, to manipulate, then to destroy or throw away when she'd gotten everything the state had wanted from him.

A voice interrupted her thoughts. It came over the airplane's speakers.

"We'll be landing at Washington National Airport in ten minutes. At this time please extinguish smoking materials and fasten your seat belts."

Mechanically the redhead snapped the belt closed around her waist and quickly reviewed her schedule for the day. It was unlikely that the men the Americans had sent to meet her would be there. They were expecting her on a later flight from London, landing at Dulles International Airport. She had changed her mind at Heathrow and switched flights at the last minute as a precautionary measure and landed at

Kennedy in New York instead. A senior intelligence officer, working under another guise in their United Nations consulate, had met her there and slipped the handgun she'd requested into the luggage she planned to check.

She tried to remember his orders. "Americans are more casual than we are," he'd commented as he'd driven her from Kennedy to La Guardia airport where she would get the shuttle to Washington. "They don't wear uniforms when they're not in meetings with their superiors. So don't wear your official clothes any more than necessary. It will make them feel uncomfortable in your presence."

She was grateful for permission not to wear the drab, heavy uniform. It had been hot in New York, and the newspaper she'd read when she boarded the flight warned that the temperature was expected to exceed ninety degrees.

She tried to remember the names of the men who were meeting her. She took out the pictures the embassy official in London had handed her at the airport before her decision to switch flights. Their names were on the backs of their pictures, as well as brief biographies. Captains Lyons and Blancanales. Probably military security of some sort.

The third one, a Major Hermann Schwarz, was listed as a nuclear engineering specialist. He looked like a boringly mild man.

She'd had her fill of both kinds recently. The bright ones were meek and the tough ones were stupid. Someday she'd find a man who had both qualities.

She remembered Lubankov, and added to her list of qualifications the words, *and not a psychopath*.

Schwarz was the one who'd be joining her at the briefing. According to the foreign ministry representative in London, he would probably also be her personal escort, although that hadn't been confirmed yet.

She looked at his picture again. The typical scientific type. Studious, shy and introverted. He'd probably apologize for an hour when he discovered that nobody had met her at the airport.

He'd invite her to lunch or dinner, then escort her to the secure apartment the Americans had made available to her. She wondered if he'd make a pass at her. Probably not. She'd have to find out what level of classified information he had access to before she made it obvious she was receptive to whatever charms he possessed.

The thought gave her little pleasure. Nothing else she thought of, or did, made her feel any better.

Until she thought again of finding Lubankov, and what she would do to him. *That* made her feel better.

10

Gadgets drove the car he had rented onto the Arlington Memorial Bridge. He glanced at the figure of the sixteenth President of the United States seated in the Lincoln Memorial as he crossed the Potomac River to enter Virginia.

He felt uncomfortable as the olive-colored collar cut into his neck. He hated having to wear the uniform of a major, adorned with the various patches and symbols that identified him as part of the nuclear weapons development forces.

Even with the air-conditioning going full blast he could feel the perspiration run down from his armpits and onto the shirtsleeves. At least Hal had promised that when he was away from the Pentagon he could switch to jeans and a short-sleeved sport shirt. With any luck that would be in two hours.

He looked ahead at the turnoff that led to the George Washington Memorial Drive. Just past it was a monstrous five-sided structure that seemed to cover the better part of forty acres. He recognized the Indiana limestone-faced complex. The Pentagon. He'd been here before, although not for several years.

The secretary of defense, and the secretaries of the individual forces who reported to him, maintained their offices and their personal staffs at the Pentagon. Joint Chiefs of Staff were also based here. Except for the commandant of the Marine Corps and a handful of administrative branches, all military directions were issued by the nearly thirty thousand people who worked in the five rings of buildings that surrounded a huge enclosed center court.

Gadgets drove into one of the parking lots and found an empty space in an area near the main entrance marked Reserved for Military Personnel on Official Business.

He set the special card Bear had given him on the front dashboard, which gave him permission to park there, and got out. Running a finger under the stiffly pressed collar of his shirt, he straightened his tie and pulled his summer uniform jacket down. Grabbing a briefcase and his soft-sided overnight bag from the seat next to him, he started for the main entrance, nodding at the armed military guards who acknowledged his rank with salutes.

As he entered the building, Gadgets hoped he wouldn't have to walk much of the seventeen miles of corridors that ran through the Pentagon to keep his appointment with Major General Cassidy. He felt uncomfortable and wished Pol and Ironman were with him, but they had driven to Dulles International Airport to meet the Russian woman and bring her to the briefing.

"I'll take good care of her," Pol had promised with a wicked wink.

Schwarz didn't like being in the Pentagon. He knew that too many politicians were trying to run the armed forces like a political machine. He knew that politics often involved nuclear weapons. ICBMs, Tritons and Pershings were mere tokens in the game of international politics that he despised. Not that the actual weapons were in the building. Only the politicians were.

Some of the men and women in this building had the ability to influence the beginning of a chain of events that could reduce the planet to little more than a huge cloud of radioactive particles. The thought gave Gadgets the shivers.

He remembered back when he was trying to decide if he should go on to college. He couldn't listen to a lecture on how nuclear fission worked without thinking of friends who were getting killed in Vietnam. What if the Vietcong or their buddies the Khmer Rouge in Cambodia got their hands on a nuclear weapon?

Despite the antiwar demonstrations and pressure from radical left-wing student groups, his conscience had forced him to turn down a scholarship offer from Cal Tech and enlist.

Gadgets had gotten himself assigned to a Special Operations Group, an elite team of men who handled only the most dangerous special missions. There had been times, hiding in the jungles, listening to friends begging him to kill them so that they wouldn't have to suffer the excruciating pain of their wounds, when he wished he was still hanging around Cal Tech listening to another boring professor ramble through another boring lecture.

This wasn't one of those times. He hadn't joined Able Team to sit through briefings. Not when there were decent men like Richard Levinson to be avenged.

He looked ahead and saw the uniformed guard who stood behind the barrier gaze at him with a bored expression.

"I have an appointment with Major General Cassidy," Gadgets replied quietly, handing him the ID card Bear had given him.

At the mention of the general's name, the guard's expression changed to one of suspicion. "What's your name?" he asked, making it clear he didn't trust the uniformed officer standing on the other side of the barrier.

"Major Hermann Schwarz."

The elderly man studied him again for a moment, then dialed the phone. "This is Lieutenant Mosten at the front desk," he said into the phone. "There's a Major Schwarz down here who says he's got an appointment with General Cassidy."

The skeptical look had disappeared from his face as he hung up and looked at Gadgets. He took out a red badge and clipped it to the Able Team warrior's jacket pocket. "Red means top-security clearance..." he started to say, then caught himself, and added lamely, "but of course *you* know that." He remembered something. "You can take your briefcase in after I check it, but you're going to have to check the suitcase."

Gadgets glanced at the metal detector machine through which he had to pass and decided it was just as well he couldn't carry the small bag to the briefing. He handed it to the elderly guard, who opened a metal door under the counter and placed it inside. Handing Schwarz a plastic tag stamped with a number, he said, "Turn that in when you leave to get your bag back."

Gadgets knew that if the man opened the suitcase he would sound the alarm and have armed guards take him into custody until he could contact someone to clear him. In the bag, along with his clothes and toiletries was one of the new Colt Delta Elite 10 mm automatics loaded with the hot new .40-caliber hollowpoint rounds he'd been testing. There were also three extra magazines loaded with the powerhouse cartridges, ready to feed into the automatic in under two seconds.

He couldn't resist substituting it for his usual weapon, the Colt Government Model automatic, not when the 170-grain rounds in the magazine slammed out of the muzzle at an awesome thirteen hundred feet per second, almost twice the muzzle energy of his favorite .45-caliber ACP.

He thought of Ironman and his insistence on sticking to his .357 Magnum Colt Python revolver. It bothered Gadgets that after only six shots his partner was what law-enforcement officers called "dead in the water" while he reloaded his weapon. It was fortunate that the muscular blond commando was deadly accurate so that he rarely needed more than a cylinder of rounds to turn a nest of psycho killers into raw hamburger.

But Gadgets put Ironman out of his mind as another guard led him down the seemingly endless corridor to the third bank of elevators and pushed the up button. After they got off the elevator on the fifth floor, the guard led the way down a wide hall until they reached a high metal fence guarded by two armed soldiers.

"This is as far as I'm allowed to go, Major," he apologized, saluting Gadgets. Before Schwarz could salute back, the man had turned and walked back to the elevators.

Gadgets hesitated for a moment, wondering what to do, when one of the guards saluted him and said, "If you'll go down the corridor to Room 320-120, General Cassidy is waiting for you, Major."

Returning the salute, he walked down the corridor. The farther he went, the more something nagged at Schwarz. He couldn't give it a label until he reached the thick wooden door with the general's name on it. Then he knew what it was.

For as busy a place as the Pentagon was supposed to be, he hadn't seen another person in the hallway since he'd gotten directions from the guards. He asked the uniformed man with two silver stars mounted on the shoulders of his open military jacket about the lack of traffic after the captain who'd escorted him into the general's large office had left.

"I'm what the Japanese would call a national treasure," the smiling man—the brass plate on his desk said his name was Major General Timothy Cassidy—answered without vanity. "Guess I know more about what we have, we can do and are planning to do in nuclear weaponry than anybody in the country." He made a face. "Talk about a lousy way to become unique."

Cassidy was tall and skinny, too thin to have ever gone through the strenuous military training Schwarz still remembered after all these years. The steel-gray hair, looking as if it badly needed cutting, hung over a pair of small, wire-framed oval eyeglasses, making the general look more like a laboratory dweller than a military officer.

Gadgets was curious. "What would happen if somebody tried to kidnap you to get you to talk?"

The general hesitated, then decided to reply. "Guess it's okay to tell you, since obviously the main man trusts you enough to let you come into our nuclear playpen." He opened his mouth to reveal a perfect set of teeth. "There's a filling in one of these teeth that I can kick out with my tongue. Guaranteed to send me on a permanent visit to my ancestors in seconds." His smile was relaxed, the smile of someone who had lived close to death for a long time.

Gadgets didn't allow himself to let first reactions interfere with his developed instinct to be cautious. But the general was someone he immediately liked. More importantly, someone he respected.

There was humor and power flashing from the man's black eyes set deeply into sockets. He looked ten years younger than the sixty-year-old Schwarz suspected he was.

Cassidy extended his hand across the desk. The Able Team warrior got a grip on it and started to shake it when he felt the general's strength. He tried to squeeze back but realized it was useless. Finally he looked down at their clasped hands. Cassidy smiled apologetically and let go.

"Sorry about that," Cassidy said. "I used to be a weight lifter in my younger years before I let this body of mine go soft."

Gadgets studied the man again. Under the thin frame he knew there had to be developed muscles. "Now you're just an arm twister," he replied, grinning. He flexed his fingers to see if they had any feeling left in them. "Or hand crusher."

The General looked pleased as he pointed at the large leather chair in front of his desk. Gadgets sat down as the senior officer came out from behind his desk and leaned against the edge. He studied the Able Team warrior.

"Now what's this about, Major... or should I say *Mr.* Schwarz, if that's your real name?"

The younger man looked around the room. Cassidy watched him and smiled gently. "This room is so bug free even the roaches have to get Q clearance to get in here."

Gadgets wondered how much the general had been told. He decided to ask him.

"Just to expect someone early this morning who would help make sure the first verifications went off without a hitch," Cassidy replied.

"That's about all I can tell you," Gadgets said apologetically.

"I was afraid you'd say something like that. Are you really military, or one of those intelligence types?" He held up his hand. "Never mind. You wouldn't tell me the truth if you were CIA." He lifted himself off the edge of the desk and stared at Gadgets. "So how can I help you?"

"First of all, I'm curious about how you feel about dismantling these missiles."

A faraway look crept into the general's eyes. "I don't think anybody's ever asked me that before, not even over at the Department of Energy where I used to work or here at the Pentagon since they gave me a rank and permanently loaned me to the GI types." He reexamined Gadgets. "Damnedest question for a CIA man to ask. Didn't think your kind cared how somebody felt."

"If it'll make you feel better," Schwarz said quietly, "I'm not from the CIA."

The older man studied Gadgets, then nodded his acceptance of the statement. "Your saying that would scare the hell out of some of the people around here," he warned. He moved back behind his desk and sat down in his well-worn leather chair. Turning the chair so that he faced the window, the general stared out at Washington, "To answer your question, some of the African tribes have a saying. When two elephants fight, it's the grass that suffers." He turned and looked at Schwarz. "If you get my drift."

"Loud and clear, General," Gadgets said with sincere admiration.

"Don't misunderstand me. I don't trust the Russians any more than anybody else around this place. But maybe this time they mean it about not wanting to turn this planet into one big hunk of charred meat." He made a face. "Like the main man said, 'Trust but verify.' If we can make sure they're keeping their end of the bargain and they can make sure we're doing the same, it's worth a try."

"That's pretty open-minded for somebody who's responsible for making sure we're staying up-to-date with our nukes," Gadgets said, sounding surprised.

"Hey, I make sure they're made properly. Somebody else—hopefully someone who hasn't flipped his wig—decides when and against whom to use them," Cassidy replied quickly. "That's the worst part of it, having to decide when to use them." A sad expression crossed his face. "I was seven years old when we dropped the A bomb on Hiroshima. But I can still remember getting sick when I heard my dad saying how many lives we were saving by killing a hundred thousand Japanese." A wry smile crossed his face. "Funny, when I decided I liked science better than baseball and got myself a scholarship to MIT, I found myself focusing my attention on the study of nuclear fission."

He studied Gadgets's face for some reaction. Schwarz forced himself to remain expressionless.

"Ironic, isn't it, that I wanted to become an expert in the thing that turned my stomach the most?" He sighed. "The Irish always were a self-destructive race." He paused and searched his memory. "They must be, or why would I have joined the Army? There I was at MIT teaching and some top-brass government types came around and offered me a job that paid twice what I was earning as an assistant professor." He laughed loudly as he remembered something. "I told them to go—" He caught himself, then continued. "But they knew how to get my Irish up. They asked if I'd rather have some soldier who liked to keep his finger on the button heading up the nuclear weapons development program instead of me." He threw his hands open as a gesture of surrender. "So I let them suck me in." He stood up from his chair. "And I've been here ever since." Smiling, he touched the side of his nose with a finger. "But I've made them do a little nervous dancing now and then. Like back in the Vietnam days."

He stopped suddenly and started to ask, "Did you happen to serve in Viet—?" Glancing at the cold expression in Gadgets's eyes, he stopped and commented, "Yeah, you did. One day some political appointee with a bunch of dead brain cells called me into his office and asked if I thought the use of nuclear weapons would help us win."

"What did you say, General?"

A boyish grin appeared on the Irishman's face. "As I remember, I told him I'd take the mercury out of a rectal thermometer, fill it with with radioactive chemicals and shove it up his ass if he brought the subject up again." He winked. "He never did."

Gadgets laughed. He liked the general. He regretted not being able to tell him anything about the assignment.

"So," Cassidy said, standing up and sounding business-like, "why have you honored us with your presence, Major Schwarz? I may as well call you that since I don't get the impression you're going to tell me your real name, right?"

Gadgets smiled and nodded. "I'm supposed to sit in on the briefing you're going to give the visiting Russian major."

"You're a deeper man than that, Major Schwarz. I don't know exactly who you really are, but you've got to be pretty damn important," the general said, concentrating his focus on Gadgets's eyes.

"What makes you say that, General?"

Cassidy relaxed. "Army majors don't usually attend private briefings from a general."

"Probably somebody just trying to make me feel at home."

The general sniffed the air. "Funny, I didn't know we had cows running around this place."

Schwarz laughed at the remark.

"Sure you're not Irish?" Cassidy added.

Gadgets shook his head. "No one is more sorry than me that I'm not, General."

"Probably a good thing for the Irish. They couldn't stand two of us in the same race." He stood up and made it clear that the meeting was ended. "Let me make one thing clear to you, Major. I intend for this dismantling to happen, no matter what it takes. Even if I'm in the minority around here."

Gadgets got to his feet. "I'm on your side, General." He checked his watch. "But I'd better get going if I'm going to meet the major and her escort."

Cassidy looked surprised. "Her escort?" He broke into laughter. "I see nobody tells you anything, either. She's waiting for us in the conference room. She got here before you did."

Gadgets thought about Ironman and Pol searching through the crowds of arrivals, looking for a specific redhead and never finding her. He grinned as he imagined their reaction when they found out it was all in vain.

"You don't seem too bothered by the news," the general said.

"Not as much as two other people I know will be," Schwarz replied, still grinning.

11

The two uniformed Army captains being dropped off in front of the arrivals section at Dulles International Airport didn't look out of place. In fact, it would have been hard to pay attention to them with the constant parade of men, women and children pushing by them to get in and out of the huge structure. Summer was the time of year when almost everyone deserted the District of Columbia and went to a less suffocating climate.

Dressed in summer tans with captains' bars on their epaulets and ribbons of past military honors, the two soldiers paused outside and began searching for someone. As they studied the area, everything appeared to be normal. Most of the unattended vehicles were crowded into the vast parking lots. The few that were parked closer to the entrance were mostly limousines, either private, or those that could be hired by the hour or day. Near them was a long line of cabs waiting for fares, their drivers standing outside, gabbing with one another to pass the time.

A small van sat at the curb near the limousines. The driver sat behind the wheel, smoking a cigarette and reading a newspaper. A company called the Federal Messenger Service owned the vehicle according to the words painted in bright blue on its side. Every now and then the driver glanced at the front doors, apparently watching for someone to appear.

"This uniform's killing me," Lyons muttered to Pol, who was walking next to him. "Especially with the Kevlar underneath."

"As long as that's the only thing," Blancanales replied in a low voice. "We've got to talk to Cowboy about coming up with a way to make the vests cooler."

Ironman nodded and kept looking around. "Something smells wrong," he commented.

"It's these uniforms," Pol said, straightening his jacket. "I can smell the camphor balls." He made a face. "I wonder what old attic Bear got them from."

Ironman kept searching for anything that might seem out of the ordinary, then finally gave up. "You ready to rock and roll just in case?"

Pol reached down and checked his right shoelace, then lightly patted his ankle. "Just call me Ready Freddy."

Because of the tight-fitting uniform Blancanales couldn't carry his favorite handgun, the Colt Government .45 ACP that Cowboy had modified to hold an extra round. But the Able Team armorer had provided him with a .38 Colt Agent revolver made of lightweight magnesium with a two-inch barrel. Pol had loaded the weapon with six rounds of Glasser cartridges, designed to penetrate through hard surfaces as if they were butter, then stop when they hit soft tissue.

The energy transfer of the specialized cartridge was almost total on short-range contact. As a result, the compact weapon, which Pol wore in a nylon holster held to his ankle by Velcro straps, had the stopping power of a .357 Magnum revolver. As a precaution, the wavy-haired warrior carried two speedloaders filled with Glasser rounds on his belt.

Ironman refused to surrender the security of his huge .357 Magnum Cold Python to the limitations of the uniform he was forced to wear. The powerful weapon was mounted in a breakaway leather holster on his belt and tucked into the small of his back. Lyons had opened the back seam of the uniform jacket so that he could grab the huge weapon instantly, and he had shoved a pair of speedloaders for the gun in his pockets, spoiling the uncreased facade he was supposed to present.

Pol led the way into the terminal building, looking around, then turned to Lyons. "Seems calm enough."

Lyons was still wary. "Too calm."

He looked around and spotted a bank of doors marked Restricted Area. Do Not Enter. From past experience he knew that the immigration and customs inspection areas lay behind the doors. Gesturing for Pol to follow him, he walked past them and stopped at a heavy metal door marked Authorized Personnel Only. "I'll bring her out," he told Blancanales in a quiet voice. "You make sure no one's waiting for us."

"Alive, you mean," Pol replied.

"Yeah, that's what I mean."

He reached into his jacket pocket and took out the special federal security pass that gave him access to the most restricted government areas. He'd have to remember to show it to the Russian officer just in case she forgot how he looked.

He paused at the door and took out the small photograph of the Russian officer that Brognola had given each of them. He had to admit she was reasonably attractive. Her nose was a little too pointed for his taste, and her chin a little too arrogant. Probably used to snarling orders, he decided, making a mental note to stay as patient as possible when she tried to order him about. He was glad Gadgets was stuck being her personal bodyguard.

A female voice kept announcing the arrival and departure of international flights over the speaker system. "TWA Flight 206 from London has landed. Those meeting arriving passengers should wait for them outside the customs area."

That was her flight, according to the information the Able Team chief of operations had given them. Ironman knocked on the door. A bald, uniformed customs supervisor opened it and glared at him from inside. "This is a restricted government area," the officious-sounding civil servant snarled. But the glare was quickly replaced by a subservient expression as the official examined the pass

Ironman handed him. "What can I do for you?" he asked, suddenly pulling in his horns.

Lyons explained that he was supposed to meet a representative of the Russian government, arriving on Flight 206.

"Want me to announce her name?"

The Stony Man warrior shook his head. "Call too much attention to her."

"Well, they're just coming into customs from that flight. Signal me when you spot her and I'll get her right through the system."

Lyons nodded, then leaned against a wall and watched as long lines of men, women and children walked through the immigration lines and into the vast open area to retrieve their luggage from the moving carousel. With the help of skycaps they dragged their baggage to one of the three customs stations and opened them for inspection.

There was no one remotely resembling the Russian in the restricted area. He moved his eyes to the entrance. People were still wandering in.

Then he saw a redheaded woman across the wide room. For a moment he thought it was the Russian major, then he studied her face. No, only the the glowing copper-colored hair was the same. This woman's features were softer, more flattened.

Disappointed he turned away and watched as the remaining passengers trickled into the inspection area. Finally the trickle of arrivals stopped. Shrugging, Lyons waved his thanks to the customs supervisor and walked through the doors to the main lobby.

A large crowd was gathered outside the exit doors from the customs area, waiting for passengers. Lyons looked around for Pol. As he did, he noticed two thickset men wearing delivery service uniforms who kept staring at the doors that led from the restricted area. One of them kept looking down at something in his hand.

There was something unpleasantly familiar about the men. Ironman glanced at them again. He had never seen their faces before, but he knew the type—syndicate street soldiers.

He wondered who they were waiting for. A Mafia big shot returning from Europe?

Maybe Pol and he should check into it. He looked around and saw Blancanales leaning against a nearby wall, staring with admiration at a striking young brunette.

Lyons whistled softly. Blancanales slowly turned away from the woman and joined him. "Find her?" he asked.

"She wasn't on the flight," Ironman said, then nudged his partner and directed his attention toward the two thugs. "Dirtbags?" he asked.

Pol nodded. "Absolutely."

"Maybe we should stick around and see who they're waiting for," Ironman suggested, touching the weapon he was wearing under his uniform.

"Better call the chief first," Blancanales suggested.

Ironman hesitated. He hated walking away from scum like the two he had spotted. Finally he shook his head in reluctant agreement and walked to a nearby pay phone to call Stony Man Farm.

Politician followed him and waited while he made the sequence of cutaway calls that finally got him through to Brognola. As Lyons made the call, Pol noticed the red-headed woman following a skycap who was pushing a handcart filled with her luggage. He tapped Lyons on the shoulder. The two thugs were walking behind her.

Suddenly Brognola came on the line, and Lyons started to explain that the Russian officer hadn't been on the flight, but the operations chief interrupted. "She took an earlier flight from New York. She's at the Pentagon, attending the briefing with Schwarz. So get your asses back here," he ordered.

Ironman told Brognola about the two hoodlums they'd spotted.

"I'll have the FBI alerted. You stay out of it," he snapped.

"Forget it. They're leaving the terminal alone," Lyons replied.

"Good. Now you've only got one thing to worry about. Getting back here before you get into trouble," Brognola said briskly, and told him where the helicopter from Stony Man Farm would meet them.

Before Ironman could ask any questions, the Able Team chief hung up. Lyons passed the news on to Blancanales. As they walked to the front doors, Pol complained, "How come we hardly ever get to stick around nice places like this?"

Before Lyons could reply, he looked out onto the sidewalk and saw the two street hoodlums dragging the terrified redhead toward the van. The gorilla with Neanderthal features had his huge muscle-heavy arms around her waist, half carrying, half dragging her toward the cab of the van.

"You're making a mistake!" she shouted in terror as he leaned over to whisper something to her. "My husband's a congressman," she screamed, sounding even more frightened.

A small group of travelers began to gather in a wide circle around the woman and the two hard-faced men. Nobody moved to rescue her, not against the obviously violent pair of kidnappers.

Finally the elderly skycap who had accompanied the woman began to protest. "You shouldn't be doing that," he yelled.

The second thug, a thin, nervous young man, pulled out a 9 mm Smith & Wesson Model 59 double-action automatic from under his uniform jacket and fired four soft-nosed slugs into the airport employee's chest. As the skycap fell in a pool of his own blood, the stunned crowd dispersed in every direction.

A young airport cop ran up the walkway in response to the loud explosions and jerked a .38 Police Special from the black leather holster on his belt. "What's going on here?" he demanded as he pointed the gun at the thin killer.

From the cab of the van the driver shoved an Ingram MAC-11 out of the open window and pulled the trigger in answer. Two short bursts of slugs tore across the policeman's waist, nearly slicing him in half. A half-dozen empty brass shells bounced off the concrete pavement while the crowd of men and women moved farther back, too frozen with fear to run.

"Get a move on!" the heavyset driver of the delivery van yelled at the two killers.

From inside the van Ironman and Pol could hear the hysterical screams of the woman. As Lyons charged the twenty feet that separated him from the van, he reached under the back of his Army uniform jacket to grab his .357 Python. "Die, dirtbag!" he shouted as he pulled the trigger, releasing an authoritative-sounding pair of rounds.

The hoodlum tried to pull the trigger of his Desert Eagle, then looked down at his hand and saw that the lead from Ironman's revolver had chewed his fingers into bone fragments and flayed skin.

While the thin, nervous thug looked unsure about what do to next, the driver shoved his weapon out the open window and closed a finger against the trigger. A pair of shots exploded in Ironman's ears. Two scorching slugs from behind Lyons tore into the gunman's face, disintegrating the ugly features into a mass of frothing blood, bone splinters and splattering viscera. What was left of the man's head slumped out of sight into the cab of the van as the MAC-11 clattered onto the roadway.

Lyons glanced quickly over his shoulder. Pol had fired from a kneeling position. In his right hand was the compact Colt revolver he had torn from its Velcro bindings around his ankle. The Glasser rounds he'd used had sliced through the killer's layers of epidermal material and shed their plastic coverings as they'd exploded inside his head, scattergunning hundreds of pellets throughout the skull cavity.

The crowd moved farther away from the van as they saw the two Army officers shooting at the trio of killers. The remaining gunman suddenly panicked and jumped inside the van. He shoved the dead man's body out the door and dragged the woman to his side.

"Let her go!" Ironman yelled as Pol moved closer to the curb.

The frightened killer shoved the hysterical woman in front of him. "I'll blow her away if you don't get out of here!" he threatened.

Blancanales muttered a Spanish curse as they heard the thug shout at the woman. The delivery van pulled away from the driveway as the killer leaned out his window and showered the area with 9 mm parabellum slugs.

The Able Team commandos scattered to avoid the ricocheting lead. Then Blancanales turned and looked around for Ironman. He saw him and quickly realized that blood was seeping through the shoulder of Lyons's military jacket. "You okay?" he asked.

The blond warrior was too busy looking around to reply. He raced to one of the limousines waiting at the curb, shoved the stunned uniformed driver standing beside it away and slid behind the wheel.

Blancanales understood Lyons's action. He dashed after him, rolling himself across the front hood to get to the other side as Lyons started the engine. Yanking the front passenger door open, Pol hauled himself inside as Ironman threw the luxurious vehicle into gear and stomped on the gas pedal.

Any other time Pol would have made a crack about having to literally "haul ass," but this wasn't the time. A woman's life was at stake.

As Ironman set new speed records racing down the driveway to catch up with the van, Pol reloaded his revolver with fresh Glasser rounds. He looked down and saw a box of facial tissues on the floor. Reaching down, he grabbed a thick stack, folded them into a wad and shoved it under Ironman's jacket to stanch the bleeding. "Want me to drive?"

"No thanks. But I'd appreciate your reloading my piece," he replied, concentrating on trying to keep the van in his view.

Blancanales dug into Ironman's side pocket for a speed-loader. As he shoved fresh loads into the cylinder, he knew that getting Lyons's shoulder taken care of would have to wait, at least until they'd first dealt with the killer who was trying to escape with his hostage.

As they tore up the driveway, they momentarily lost sight of the van thanks to a series of curves, and Pol cursed. Then, as they rocketed onto an interstate access road, they spotted the van again. It was getting too far ahead of them. Ironman set his jaw and floored the gas pedal.

"Not good, amigo," Pol said angrily.

Lyons understood. "He's driving now. And she's probably dead."

Blackness filled the pupils of Blancanales's eyes. "So's he."

Buffeted by the air pressure its high speed was creating, the van swerved back and forth across the road as it rushed toward the interstate.

Driving in the calm pocket its movement had created behind the van, Lyons moved steadily closer. Suddenly the van swerved and raced onto a side road.

Pol read the small sign marking the road. "He's heading for Wolf Trap Farm Park."

"We'll get rid of the skunk there," Lyons said coldly as he entered the two-lane road. Then he glanced down at the dashboard. There was a mobile telephone mounted on it. "See if you can reach Stony Man."

Pol picked up the unit and punched in some numbers. Quickly he gave the coded words that told the listener this was an emergency. Skipping the usual routine, Blancanales was patched through to Bear and told him what had happened and where they were. He could hear the computer genius calling for Brognola to get on the line. The familiar voice growled, and Pol punched a button that permitted them both to talk and listen to him.

Ironman recapped the events for Brognola.

"Any chance the woman's alive?" the Stony Man chief asked.

"None," Lyons said with certainty.

"Your leg okay?" Brognola asked. They knew who he meant.

"I've been too busy to think about it," Ironman replied. "What do you want us to do?"

"You got a preference?" the voice over the speaker asked.

"Yeah," Pol answered for both of them. "Stop him!"

"Go to it," Brognola said. "I'll make sure the authorities don't delay you after you're done."

"Thanks," Lyons replied, glaring with fury at the speeding van in front of them.

"One thing," the voice warned. "No getting hurt. You've got a trip out of here tomorrow."

"Wilco," Pol promised. "Over and out." He turned to his partner. "Enough playing games. Let's ice the scum."

As if he'd only been waiting for Blancanales's suggestion, Ironman pressed down harder on the gas pedal and began to inch up on the van. Spinning almost out of control at the curves, the killer's vehicle tried to pull away. Lyons kept up the pressure, edging the limousine close to the other vehicle as he inched up. Turning the wheel gently, Ironman let his left fender make contact with the rear quarter of the delivery vehicle. The panicky thug tried to pull in front of the luxurious Cadillac. Handling the stretch limousine like a Formula One racing car, Ironman turned away from the van, then suddenly spun the steering wheel and ran a diagonal line at the front of the vehicle.

They could see the face of the frightened killer inside the cab of the van as he tried to avoid being hit. The deep, narrow ditch on his left rushed up to grab his left tires. Terrified, the street soldier tried turning back onto the roadway. But it was too late. The van rolled over onto its side.

Ironman slowed the limousine down and stopped next to the overturned vehicle. There was no movement from inside.

Pol looked at his partner. "Think he's dead?"

Lyons shoved fresh cartridges into his Colt Python and opened his door. "For his sake, I hope so."

The two men eased out of the limousine and separated as they approached the van. They stood a short distance away and listened carefully. The only sound was that of sirens coming from behind them. Pol looked questioningly at Lyons.

"Let's check it out," the blond commando said.

Carefully they moved to the passenger door of the van. As Blancanales kept his finger tight against the trigger of his revolver, Lyons twisted the handle and pulled the door open. The young hood was crushed against the steering wheel, jammed into a corner by the still-bleeding body of the redheaded woman.

"You two okay?" a Maryland State Police lieutenant asked as he came over and saw the blood seeping through Ironman's jacket.

"Better than him," Pol replied, then noticed a manila envelope on the floor of the van.

Lyons glanced down at his shoulder. "I guess I could use a Band-Aid," he admitted.

The lieutenant nodded and walked away to get a paramedic.

Pol glanced at Iron's face. He could see the pain his partner wouldn't admit to having. He reached down and picked up the envelope on the floor, then studied the photocopied pages he found inside and whistled in surprise.

"What do you think they were doing with classified information about our nuclear missile program?" he asked. Before Lyons could reply, a paramedic came over with his kit. He gently pulled away the jacket and studied the large hole in the shoulder.

"You could use some stitches," he said.

"Just a Band-Aid," Lyons insisted.

The paramedic was about to argue when he saw the don't-mess-with-me expression on Ironman's face. Instead, he opened the kit and bandaged the wound, then gave the Able Team warrior a precautionary shot of antibiotic. "Don't let it go too long," he warned.

Ironman glanced at the two body bags on the ground. "I may not get a chance for a while."

The paramedic seemed to understand. He reached into his kit and took out two small vials and handed them to Lyons. "Take the antibiotic four times a day for at least a week. The other's a simple painkiller." He looked resigned as he added, "When you find the time to admit to yourself that you're hurting."

"Thanks," Ironman said. Then he waited until the uniformed man walked away before he looked at Blancanales and asked, "Got the picture of that Russian major on you?"

Pol reached into an inside pocket and took out the color photograph. They stared at the face that looked up at them. The feature that stood out was her red hair, just like that of the dead woman in the van.

"I think Gadgets has got more trouble on his hands than he realizes," Blancanales commented.

"I think we better call Hal and convince him to let us stick around here," Lyons said, agreeing with his partner.

12

Gadgets didn't think he was in trouble when he entered the conference room behind the general, not when he saw the beautiful woman who was sitting at the large oval table, scribbling aimlessly on a yellow pad. For a moment he thought Cassidy had asked one of the better-looking secretaries to sit in on the briefing and take notes.

Then he remembered the photograph and realized that this was the Russian major. Suddenly he felt sorry for Lyons and Blancanales, who were probably on their way back to Stony Man Farm, frustrated at their wasted trip. He felt especially sorry for Pol.

The photograph Brognola had given Gadgets hadn't prepared him for what Major Tolstoy would look like in the flesh. And he could see a lot of her flesh through the thin summer frock she wore.

She glanced up at him, then turned away and reached down into the briefcase sitting on the floor next to her to take out a folder.

Gadgets could only guess at her age—somewhere from mid-twenties to early thirties. Given her rank, she was probably in her thirties. He guessed she weighed about 120 pounds, which seemed exactly right for her height; every inch of her body was perfectly proportioned.

There was something about her expression that made it clear she had come from a heritage of Tartars or Cossacks, both noted for their fierceness and love of fighting. She only wore the slightest hint of makeup, but she seemed to know how to maximize the attractiveness of her high cheekbones, velvety skin and long, thin nose. Her thick red hair, threatening to break free from the flimsy barrette that tried to hold it in place at the back of her neck, was long enough to touch the collar of her obviously expensive silk dress.

But it was her eyes that fascinated and bothered the Able Team warrior the most. There was a very smart woman behind the gray-green eyes. And there was something else there, something he couldn't easily identify.

The general broke the ice as he sat down at the far end of the long wooden conference table. "Now that we've gotten acquainted," he said, trying to contain a desire to laugh, "let me introduce you to each other." He turned to the woman. "Major, this is Major Hermann Schwarz." He turned to Gadgets. "Major Irina Tolstoy is part of the Soviet Verification Team. She flew here in advance of the rest of the group to review our plans for our first Bastille Day Party."

The Russian major stood and extended her hand to Gadgets. For a moment he stared at it, then realized she wanted him to shake hands. Looking embarrassed, he took her hand. He glanced quickly at the figure he could see outlined beneath the dress. He got the impression that she followed a daily regime of some form of aerobic exercise rather than weight lifting like Ironman. But then, he reminded himself, who wanted to go out on a date with Ironman?

Major Tolstoy stared at their still-joined hands. Quickly Gadgets pulled his hand away and sat down. Turning away from him, the Russian looked at the general and asked in an accented voice, "Bastille Day party?"

"When the French chopped off the queen's head during the French Revolution," Cassidy explained, smiling.

"Ah, revolution," the redhead replied with an expression of approval.

"I think General Cassidy was making a joke," Schwarz said, jumping in.

"Revolutions are not jokes," the major reprimanded him.

Gadgets took a deep breath and reminded himself that the Russians tended to be literal people. He wondered if any of them ever told a joke. "I think," he said to her in a tense voice, "that when the general referred to separating the queen's head from the rest of her body, he was trying to make a joke. I think," he continued, hearing himself sound like a schoolteacher repeating a lesson to a student, "he was referring to the first dismantling of our Pershing missiles."

"There is no time for jokes," she complained. "Can we get to the briefing now?"

Gadgets kept looking at her eyes. Suddenly he knew what had bothered him about her. There were no feelings reflected in them. It wasn't that she had pulled down a curtain to hide them. In their blackness he saw emptiness, and he knew that any emotions she may have ever felt had died a long time ago.

He had seen that same deadness before—in the eyes of his two partners, and in the eyes he saw when he looked into his own mirror, especially after he had just completed a particularly bloody mission. His thoughts were interrupted by the general's firm voice.

"Major Tolstoy is right, Major Schwarz. Let's get started."

Gadgets reached for a yellow pad and pen from the stack in the middle of the table and turned to look at the older man who sat at the far end of the conference table.

General Cassidy opened the large notebook he carried and extracted two sets of papers. He slid one down to the Russian woman. "This is a summary of our short-range missile inventory, here and in other countries, with a listing of where we have them and how many there are in each location. I'll take you through a review of our missile development within the conditions of the treaty. You can ask questions when I'm through. Is that understood?" He stared at the Russian major, then at Gadgets for acknowledgment.

"You sound like a Russian professor," the redhead commented, smiling for the first time since Gadgets had been in the conference room.

Gadgets couldn't stop his laugh, even when Cassidy stared at him icily. Finally the general grinned. "Ask questions whenever you have one, Major Tolstoy."

"Spasibo," she agreed.

Gadgets saw the blank expression on the Irishman's face. "She said thanks."

She looked surprised as her eyes studied Gadgets for the second time since he'd arrived. "Do you speak Russian?" she asked.

Turning to her, he admitted, "Not much. Only Russian I speak is what I picked up as a child from some kids in the neighborhood whose parents emigrated from Russia, and from spy novels where the bad guys are always Russian agents."

"I read them, too," the woman admitted, laughing easily. "But in our books it's always Americans and their satellite lackeys who are villains."

Gadgets grinned. She had a sense of humor, after all.

"I'd like to get started," the general interrupted. He began to talk, then stopped and turned to the redheaded woman. "Before I do, let me ask you a question, Dr. Tolstoy. As a scientist, how do you feel about nuclear weapons?"

Automatically the Russian major began to answer with, "Of course my government has never felt—"

Cassidy stopped her. "I can read how your government feels. What I was asking was how *you* feel," he said pointedly.

The woman stared at him, puzzled for a few minutes, then lowered her head and focused her eyes on the polished wooden surface of the conference table. Finally she lifted her head and looked at him again. "What is said in this room stays in this room?" she asked.

"Of course," the general replied, then looked at Gadgets. "Agreed?" he asked him.

"Agreed," Schwarz replied, and studied the variety of emotions that passed rapidly across the Russian's face.

"I would like to see missiles vanish from the earth. Not just yours and ours, but everybody's," she replied with emotion. "There can be only one end if we continue this nuclear race. The end of life as we know it. This is no future for any sane person to want."

"I agree," Cassidy replied, looking relieved. "And thank you, Doctor. I can promise you that your opinions will never leave this room."

For more than an hour the Irishman reviewed the American plans. "Over the next three years we'll be disassembling and destroying our 860 short-term missiles. When the rest of your group arrives, we'll demonstrate, using two Pershing missiles, how we plan to conduct the dismantling. That will be out at a test site named China Lake, which is near Edwards Air Force Base in California. The actual dismantling will take place at the Longhorn Army Ammunitions Plant in Karnack, Texas."

"I believe the Navy has a weapons testing site at this China Lake," Major Tolstoy commented. Before either of the men could react, she asked another question. "These warheads, what is their exact composition?"

Cassidy shook his head. "Asked like a true scientist—or spy. I'm sorry. The terms of the treaty don't require me to answer that. But you can try that question on the DOE people who'll be attending the dismantling, since they're the ones who made the 'big-noise' component."

Gadgets started to explain what the initials stood for when the Russian officer stopped him. "I know what they stand for, Major. Your Department of Energy, which manufactures the nuclear material."

"I'll bet you do," Gadgets cracked cynically.

"Sounds like you Soviets have some good spies," Cassidy added.

"Possibly. But you Americans publish excellent reference books that provide us with much of what we need to know about your nuclear programs," she replied dryly.

"And what we don't publish you somehow manage to find out, anyway," Gadgets commented.

"Major Schwarz, that sounded like an accusation," the redhead said, pretending to be shocked. "I thought our two countries had become friendly."

"Like kissing cousins?"

She looked puzzled.

"I'll explain that to you another time."

"Tomorrow, we'll fly you to California and give you a private preview of how we're going to destroy some very expensive hardware," the general continued.

"Which is what I believe we'll be doing with the man you flew over yesterday," she replied.

Schwarz showed his surprise. Cassidy looked amused. "He left last night on a commercial flight, wearing civilian clothes. The Soviets will pick him up at the airport and fly him to Kiev."

"Where we will drive him to the Medium Machine Ministry facilities to watch how we'll dismantle our missiles," the Russian woman added.

"Which is one of the places where you also assemble them," the general retorted. "Enough chit-chat," he said sternly, and continued his lecture. Finally, after reviewing the domestic and foreign locations of the missiles, and how many were at each site, he looked at the attractive woman. "Anything else I can tell you?" he asked. Then he added, "That I'm allowed to tell you."

She glanced through her notes. "Probably nothing you'd be willing to share. Most of this we already knew."

"We figured as much," the general said, shrugging. "Which is why, I guess, I was allowed to tell it to you." He began to show his fatigue. "Any other questions?"

Gadgets glanced at the pages of notes he had taken and shook his head. He avoided looking at the Russian major for her reply. The sooner he got out of there, the more comfortable he'd feel. How could somebody so beautiful be so cold? he wondered sadly.

Cassidy turned to the Russian woman. She raised her eyes to the ceiling for a moment, then looked at the general and looked satisfied. "No. It was a very good lecture."

"Well, I've got to admit both of you asked some pretty good questions," the general said, gathering up his papers. He stood up and looked at Schwarz. "You know, with a mind like yours, you didn't have to settle for invitations from Cal Tech. You could have gotten into MIT."

There was a slight edge in her voice that surprised both Cassidy and Gadgets as the Russian major asked, "Is something wrong with Cal Tech?"

The general looked surprised. "I'm surprised you've even heard of it, Major."

She made a face and turned to Gadgets. "How do you stand such misplaced snobbery?" She glared at the Irishman. "Cal Tech is the best technical institute in the United States and the second finest in the world. Behind ours, of course."

"Don't take it personally, Major," Schwarz said.

"Then you have no loyalty to Cal Tech like me?" the Russian major asked.

"I never actually went there," Gadgets admitted. "I just sat in on some lectures."

Cassidy sounded suspicious. "Like you, Major?"

"I was sent there for two years," she said, smiling as she spoke.

Gadgets stared at her in amazement. The deadness in her eyes had suddenly vanished, replaced by a fiery mixture of anger and amusement.

"I'm out of here, as you youngsters would say." The general winked at Gadgets. "I'll leave it to you to continue the discussions." He walked out of the room and slammed the door behind him.

Gadgets and the Russian major sat across the table, trying not to stare at each other. Finally Schwarz broke the silence. "Did we ever meet on campus?"

"I'd be insulted if you didn't remember," the redhead replied, flaring her nostrils. Then she broke into a smile. "No, you had left before I got there. But I had heard tales from others who knew you about this genius who had turned down a scholarship to go fight in a foolish war."

"Vietnam wasn't—" Gadgets started to say angrily.

The Russian held up a hand. "Let us not get started on that subject. We talked it to death night after night when I was at Cal Tech, and nobody ever changed anybody else's opinions." The edges of her mouth twisted into a smile. "Just like trying to convince an American how inferior his form of government is to ours."

Gadgets started to reply, then changed his mind. He wanted to know more about what Major Tolstoy was doing here. Gadgets could accept she knew a lot about nuclear weaponry, but some sixth sense said she was much more than just a scientist. He wanted to find out. "How about some lunch instead? We can tear apart some of the professors we both knew."

She reached down and lifted her briefcase, then stood up. "I have been traveling for the past day. I think I would prefer to go to this so-called safehouse your government has promised me, take a bath and get some rest, Major. Could you have someone take me there?"

Gadgets complied and they left the conference room together. He rode down the elevator with her and waited while she handed the security guard a plastic chip and retrieved her suitcase. Turning to the elderly guard, she asked if there was a ladies' room nearby.

He pointed to the first corridor. "Just around that corner. First door."

"I'll be right back," she said, smiling at Gadgets.

After she had vanished, Schwarz turned in the plastic circle the guard had given him and waited until the elderly man found his overnight bag. Gadgets glanced at the corridor down which the major had gone. "Men's room someplace around there?"

"Right next door."

"If the Russian major comes out first, tell her to wait for me," he said as he trotted toward the men's room.

He'd just finished and reentered the corridor when the redhead walked out of the ladies' room. She looked at the door marked Men and smiled at him. "Two minds with a single purpose," she commented.

"It would seem so," Gadgets replied, feeling more secure with the 10 mm Colt auto inside his waistband. They walked side by side to the massive front doors. "I hope we can get a chance to talk before you return to Russia," Gadgets said casually.

"I don't think so. I leave Washington in the morning."

"Then maybe we can talk on the plane," Schwarz said. He noticed her expression of surprise. "I thought you knew. I've been assigned to act as your escort."

She looked impressed. "Your superiors must think very highly of you, Major Schwarz, to give you such an important responsibility to handle all alone."

He could hear the sarcasm in her voice. "I'll have help," he replied brusquely, thinking of Pol and Ironman.

The redhead's face suddenly became a mask of innocence. "Not that I don't think you can't handle our visit to your country by yourself."

"You should have tried out for the theater," Gadgets muttered bitterly.

"I did while I was at Cal Tech," she said, smiling sweetly. "Meantime," she added, making it clear she was getting tired of their verbal dueling, "since you are my escort, I would appreciate it if you would escort me to the official residence. I am told it isn't safe for a single woman to travel alone in a big, strange city."

As he held the front door open for her, he had to admit to himself that he felt sorry for any would-be mugger or rapist who might attempt to attack her.

13

The first Hollings learned of the fiasco at the airport was when he turned on the news and caught the live report from Dulles International Airport.

"To recap the story," the television reporter continued, "three gunmen failed in their attempt to kidnap Sheila Landriss, wife of Congressman Harvey Landriss of Oklahoma, at Dulles Airport this morning. All three gunmen were killed by police after they attempted to flee in a stolen van. Mrs. Landriss was killed by one of the gunmen before police could rescue her."

A picture of the slain woman was shown. Hollings stared at her red hair, furious that the men had targeted the wrong person. He assumed the classified document had been overlooked in the confusion.

But where was the Russian woman? Johnson, the only person who might know, was dead and couldn't tell him. Reluctantly he placed a call to Ruiz through the El Paso tie line and told him what had happened.

"What are you planning to do about it?" Ruiz asked quietly.

"Find the Russian major. Then kill her and plant the papers on her body."

Ruiz was a practical man. "And if that doesn't work?"

Hollings thought about it. "There's always California when the Russians arrive."

"I have faith in you, amigo," the voice said.

Hollings understood. He'd been at bat once and missed. He had two more tries. Then he was out. Permanently.

Ruiz wasn't like the KGB. He had allies everywhere. Hollings had lived on the run. He didn't want to have to do it again, not with all the money he had accumulated toward his pending retirement.

"Feel free to use the banker and his contacts," Ruiz added.

"I thought you wanted him replaced," Hollings reminded him.

He heard the sigh through the phone speaker. "We are not in full agreement, so let it go for now," the Mexican said before he hung up.

Hollings looked around the room. It was time to pack his bag and get ready to leave. He could always complete the mission in California. But things would be easier if it ended with the woman.

But where was she?

He thought about it, and realized that the only reason she would have come to Washington would be to meet with people in the Pentagon. He glanced at the clock on his night table. If she was there, she'd still be in a meeting. Americans talked forever. So did Russians.

He walked to the sliding patio door of his room. Wittsinger and one of his men were sitting in plastic webbed chairs around the tiny swimming pool on the other side of the narrow strip of grass the motel laughingly called a lawn.

Hollings called out. The German looked across at him and saw his angry expression. The scar that crossed the front of his face grew dark as he got up from his chair and signaled the other man to follow.

As he watched them move toward him, the former KGB agent decided to send Wittsinger with the others to the Pentagon. If they took her out there, he could deal with them and leave this unpleasant climate and return to Mexico City. If not, he'd have to go to California and suffer the desert heat of July. Regretfully he could think of no other options.

He dug into Johnson's briefcase and took out another document stamped Classified just as the two men came into the motel room. He told them what had happened and explained the change in plans.

THE FEELING OF IMPENDING DANGER stayed with Gadgets as he led the Russian major to where he had parked the car. He kept looking around, but could see nothing that was out of place.

He noticed Major Tolstoy looking strangely at him as he opened the passenger door and waited for her to get in before closing it. He started walking around to the driver's side, then stopped and checked out the area one more time.

Gadgets looked at everything and everyone. There was a black Lincoln waiting at the curb. Inside were two hard-faced men looking uncomfortable in their business suits.

Probably plainclothes bodyguards waiting for some big shot, he decided as he let his eyes run down the rows of parked cars in the main lot. Here and there cars were pulling in or out. No one in them seemed to be looking at him. So much for being careful, he told himself as he got into the car and started it.

The Russian woman studied his face. "Is something wrong, Major?"

Gadgets glanced over his shoulder one last time as he backed the rental car out of the space, then straightened it out and slowly exited the parking area. "Just looking to see if any old friends happened to be around," he said as casually as he could.

He turned onto the George Washington Memorial Parkway, which paralleled the slow-moving Potomac River. Still wary, Schwarz checked the traffic behind him in the rearview mirror.

It was one of the rare times when he'd lucked out. There were almost no cars on the road. Just the black Lincoln that had entered the parkway behind him.

Major Tolstoy seemed fascinated at the landmarks they passed. She pointed to a sign across the road, which read Federal Highway Administration. "We could use such a department in Russia. Our roads—even the main ones—are badly in need of repair."

Gadgets didn't bother pointing out that the sign was a cover for the real identity of the building, a CIA facility, hidden from casual view by trees, shrubbery and the innocuous sign. He changed the subject. "We'll be leaving on a military transport in the morning. Better dress lightly. It's going to be plenty hot where we're going."

"Not where I'm going," she replied. "At least not as hot as the Mojave Desert where your Edwards Air Force Base is located." She looked at the hostile expression on his face. "It has been cleared with your people," she added.

Gadgets couldn't hide his annoyance that Brognola hadn't told him Major Tolstoy was planning a side trip.

She began to laugh. "The suspicious American. And your newspapers call the Russians mistrusting!"

Schwarz clenched his teeth. If anything happened to her, he'd blow the reason for the elaborate charade. As they drove along the parkway, he decided to take the direct approach. "Where are you going?"

She started laughing again. "Cal Tech, to drop in and say hello to some of my old professors." She had a twinkle in her eye as she asked, "Since you are my official escort, would you care to come along, Major?"

Gadgets felt a sense of relief. "I thought you'd never ask." Some of the tension he'd been feeling began to ease. "I'm not very good at playing private detective and trying to follow you without being found out."

"That's right," she replied lightly, "James Bond was an Englishman, not an American."

Her teasing didn't seem to bother him, now that he wasn't burdened by that heavy feeling he'd had. He wondered if its disappearance had something to do with the emerging warmth between them. He glanced at her quickly, then turned his eyes back to the road. He hoped so.

Idly he looked in the rearview mirror. The boat-long Lincoln was still behind them. Gadgets wondered when it was going to exit the parkway. The wariness returned. He decided to slow down and see if it passed him, but it maintained its position behind him.

Glancing back, he saw the two expressionless men in the front seat of the car. For a moment he wondered if Brognola had sent them to keep an eye on him. No, that didn't make sense. If Brognola was going to send anybody, it would be Pol or Ironman.

Gadgets wondered who the two were. Trying not to alarm the major, he eased the 10 mm Colt automatic out of his waistband and tucked it between his legs.

It might just be his imagination, he reminded himself, but there was one way to find out. He checked the road ahead of him. Traffic was fortunately almost nonexistent. Only one car—a small Toyota sedan—was coming toward him on the opposite side of the road. There were no cars behind the Lincoln.

Leaning his head forward, he pushed down hard on the gas pedal. The midsize rental car tore ahead in response to the surge of gasoline-generated energy.

The Russian major was shoved back by the sudden acceleration. She started to ask a question, then stopped when she saw the grim expression on his face. Instead, she turned her head and looked out the rear window.

Glancing in the side mirror, Gadgets saw the large dark vehicle moving quickly to catch up to them. Now he knew. The Russian major and he were the targets. Or, at least, one of them was.

He could slam on the brakes, jump out and try to eliminate the two men following him. But there was always the chance that a stray slug would hit the Russian redhead.

The risk was too great. He'd have to outrun them. He could hear the protesting squeal of tires behind him as the other driver tried to keep up with his erratic bursts of speed.

The woman turned quickly from the rear window and looked at Gadgets. "What are they holding out the window?"

He glanced in his rearview mirror. There was a flash of reflected sunlight bouncing off a metal object being held out of the front window of the car behind him. He couldn't make out what kind of gun it was at that distance. Probably an Uzi or TEC-9. Street rats seemed to prefer them.

He didn't waste time worrying about the manufacturer. It didn't matter. Any one of them could kill.

Over the rush of wind slamming against his car, he could hear the soft thud of slugs glancing off his vehicle. The chunks of hot lead cut grooves into the skin of the car as Gadgets kept trying to present as small a profile as he could to them. He suspected the rental agency would be lucky to get back a vehicle that was only scarred by streaks of searing slugs.

He didn't have time to worry about it now. He'd let Brognola or Bear work out a settlement with them. He had enough to do trying to keep his passenger and himself alive.

Gadgets decided to try another tactic. He jammed down on the brakes. The Lincoln almost slammed into his rear, then swerved and moved parallel to his window.

Steering with his right hand, Schwarz grabbed the 10 mm automatic in his left hand and shoved it out his window at the other vehicle. As he emptied his clip, he saw the wide-faced man framed in the opened window drop his automatic pistol and grab for his face, then heard him shriek at the sudden pain.

Gadgets couldn't risk an accident by taking his eyes off the road. Guessing at the direction, he rapidly pumped two more rounds at the sound of the screaming man. He heard the plinking sound of brass cases bouncing against his door, and the high-pitched whine as one of the slugs ricocheted from the edge of the window deep into the man's left eye.

As Gadgets risked glancing at the car briefly, he saw the man slide down out of view. Cowboy was right, Gadgets decided. The new Colt was one hell of a killing machine.

The driver raised a squat, ugly automatic pistol in his right hand and started firing wildly at him. Gadgets tried to return the fire, then heard the ominous metallic click as the Colt's hammer hit metal.

There was no time to drop the clip and snap in a new one. All he could do was try to outrun the other car. As he started to crouch forward, he was stunned to hear Major Tolstoy shout, "Lean back!"

He felt a burning tail of hot lead rush past his face as he pushed his head against the rest on his seat, then heard the ringing sound of two 9 mm parabellum slugs coming from his right. They flew through the open window and hit the narrow metal trim around the other vehicle's window.

He glanced at the Russian woman and saw the compact Walther P-5 automatic she was steadying in her hands. Her eyes were hard, shiny balls of light focused on the car to his left. All Gadgets could do to help was to keep the two cars parallel.

"Hang on, Major!" he yelled as he twisted the steering wheel from one side to another, trying to close the gap between the two vehicles. Out of the corner of his eye he saw the redhead fire three more of the eight shots in the German automatic's magazine.

The driver of the Lincoln slumped forward, as if he had just decided he needed to take a nap. The driverless luxury car started to swerve out of control.

"Brace yourself," Gadgets shouted as he slammed on the brakes and let the other car pull ahead.

Like an enraged elephant, the Lincoln went berserk, twisting its way in a figure-eight motion across the road, narrowly missing a station wagon coming in the opposite direction. As Schwarz and the major watched, the metallic behemoth crashed at full speed into a wire barrier on the edge of the road and stopped momentarily. Then, suddenly, the gas tank ruptured and exploded into a brilliant ball of flame. A body flew through the space that had once held a front windshield and rolled across the highway, stopping a few feet from the rental car.

Gadgets shoved open his door and started getting out, then remembered his weapon was empty. Quickly dropping the empty clip onto the floor of the car, he snapped in a fresh magazine and jumped out. He heard the other door open. The Able Team warrior watched the major snap another magazine into the butt of the Walther as they cautiously approached the still form on the ground.

Schwarz nudged the body with a toe, aiming his Colt at it in case the gunman was only feigning death. Too many of his friends had been killed in Vietnam by just such a ploy by the VC. Satisfied the gunman was dead, he kneeled and turned him over. What remained of the face was covered with blood-soaked dirt. Much of the neck had been shot away. He looked at the overturned car and saw the other body trapped inside the twisted metal. Then he turned and glanced at the Russian major. Her face revealed no emotions, although he sensed she was satisfied.

He understood how she must feel. He had felt the same way many times. Killing was an ugly but necessary part of his job. He didn't have to like doing it. But when it had to be done, better that it was him doing it to someone else than someone else doing it to him.

It was the philosophy of professionals who sometimes had to kill in the line of duty. It was his philosophy, Pol's philosophy, Ironman's philosophy. And, he now knew, it was the Russian woman's philosophy. Whatever else she pretended to be, she was a professional like the three of them. No better. And perhaps no worse.

They heard sirens in the distance. He tapped her arm and pointed to the battered rental car. They got in and drove away before the police arrived and detained them for questioning.

Neither one of them spoke as Gadgets pointed the vehicle in the direction of the safehouse. There wasn't anything to say. At least not until they found out which one of them had been the target. And why.

14

From behind the closed door Gadgets could still hear the sounds of the shower pounding slugs of water incessantly as if it were set on autoburn. The victim of that assault was willingly submitting herself to the torture of the sharp, burning needle points shooting out from the shower head. Hot needle points, Gadgets decided as he watched steam seep out from under the bottom of the doorway from the vantage point of the small couch in the living room of the safehouse.

He had chosen to shower first while the major sorted through her suitcase. A quick cold shower had rinsed the sour smell of death from his body. Unlike a hot shower, it had invigorated him.

Wrapped in a large towel, he had come out twenty minutes ago and dripped his way into his bedroom while the major had gone into the bathroom and locked the door. He glanced at the uniform Bear had provided him and chose instead to put on a pair of Levi's and a thin work shirt that he often wore.

Refreshed, and unrestrained by the facade of the military costume, Gadgets felt he was ready for anything. He felt under the shirt for the Delta Elite he had tucked into his waistband. Pressing against his Kevlar bulletproof undershirt, it felt no different than the weapon he usually carried—the .45 ACP Colt Government auto.

Gadgets knew that not even the body armor Cowboy had recently created would afford him better protection than the standard item issued to law-enforcement agencies. There was nothing that could guarantee he'd reach the age where he could collect Social Security.

Shit, Gadgets commented silently. Who wanted to?

Before he could continue his reflections, he heard the lock on the bathroom door turn. The door opened and the Russian major, her hair covered with a towel and wearing a huge bath sheet around her body, came out. She glanced around and saw him looking at her. Smiling, she disappeared into the bedroom she had selected as hers and closed the door without saying a word.

There was a perfume in the air. Gadgets wasn't sure if it was something she'd sprayed on herself or her natural odor. It was sweet and very feminine. Probably from a bottle, he decided, remembering how she had handled a gun.

He studied the apartment the CIA had lent Stony Man. Like so many government facilities, it had no personality. The couch, the chairs, the tables, the rug were bland, as if whoever had decorated the unit was afraid to take a position—even on colors.

Still, he reminded himself, it was clean, comfortable and—most importantly—unlisted as a government property. From the outside it looked like any detached town house in a suburban Virginia lower-middle-class neighborhood. There was no garage, just two bedrooms, two baths, a combined living and dining room, and a tiny fireplace. And air conditioners, which Gadgets had turned on while the Russian woman was taking her shower.

She finally came out of the bedroom wearing a long silklike kimono as she ran a brush leisurely through her thick hair. "I haven't eaten a decent meal since I left Moscow," she said.

"We could go out," he offered. There was a folder in the small house, listing the restaurants nearby.

"After the encounter this morning, I'm not sure that would be very smart."

Gadgets had searched through the cabinets in the kitchen. They were empty. So was the refrigerator. "We could order something in,'' he suggested. He remembered seeing a listing for a Chinese restaurant that delivered.

"That makes more sense," she said, sitting down next to him.

"Any kind of food you like better than others?"

She thought about it. "Yes. Pizza. With lots of cheese, sausage, mushrooms and green peppers," she said with a expression of ecstasy, as if she were already tasting the food.

Gadgets had to admit that the redhead was full of surprises.

She saw him looking confused. "And make sure it's a deep dish pizza, like we used to get delivered at Cal Tech," she added, laughing as she jumped up and ran into her bedroom.

Still surprised at her request, Gadgets got up and searched for the list of restaurants. It was hidden in the stack of magazines on the table. He ran his finger down the list until he came to a pizzeria that offered delivery service.

He sensed her coming up behind him and looking over his shoulder as he picked up the telephone and dialed the number.

"Do you deliver?" he asked into the phone.

"Yeah, but we're running late. Can't promise getting a pizza to you in less than ninety minutes or maybe two hours," the male voice said.

"Is it deep dish pizza?" the redhead yelled into the phone from behind Gadgets.

"Tell the lady yes," the man said, laughing.

Schwarz turned his head and looked at her. "Can you hold out for two hours?"

She nodded. "For a decent pizza, absolutely."

He turned back and completed the order, then hung up and looked at her. "What would you like to do until it gets here?"

She painted an expression of innocence on her face. "We could talk about what you really do for a living," she said coyly.

Gadgets shook his head.

"You're not one of those mercenaries available for hire by anybody willing to pay them?"

"My problem is I don't get paid enough."

"Ah, then you must work for the government."

"Enough about me," Gadgets said. "I'd rather hear what your job really is."

"You don't believe I am just a dedicated nuclear scientist?"

"I think you probably know a lot about the subject. But, no, I think you're a lot more than a scientist."

Major Tolstoy shrugged. "I guess that kills that area of conversation." She thought for a moment. "You wouldn't like to talk about why those men were trying to kill you?"

"Or you," the Able Team warrior replied.

"Me?" The major looked surprised. "Why would anyone want to kill me?"

Gadgets plopped himself down on the couch and locked his hands behind his head. "I can think of at least three reasons."

"Really? Name them," she challenged.

"First, somebody doesn't like you."

"That's a possibility," she admitted. "But most of them are dead or in a Russian prison."

"Or somebody doesn't like the company you're keeping these days," Gadgets continued.

"Namely you?"

"Specifically me."

"But our two countries are almost friends," she said, maintaining the half-kidding tone both had been using.

"And somebody may not like that."

She thought about it. "That's a possibility."

"A probability," Schwarz replied. "Given the fact that transports loaded with nuclear experts from both our countries were sabotaged."

The semimocking expression vanished from the red-head's face as she considered Gadgets's comment. She nodded in agreement, then sat down next to him. "You said there were three reasons. What's the third?"

"You were with me and they didn't want witnesses."

She studied his face. "Are you that dangerous?"

"Actually, I'm one of the sweetest men I know," Gadgets said. "And..." he started to add, then changed his mind and stopped.

"And what?" Major Tolstoy sounded irritated that he hadn't finished the thought.

He grinned at her. "And you can ask my mother if you don't believe me."

She howled in frustration and tried to punch him in his arm. Schwarz twisted his body so that she missed and fell onto the couch behind him. Her head touched his right side. She rubbed her head slowly against his side, then sat up. "You expecting company?" she asked.

"I hope not."

She flipped his shirt up and exposed the Delta Elite tucked into his waistband. "Then why the gun?"

Gadgets stood and let his shirt fall over the automatic. "My mother raised a nice guy, not a stupid one."

"Meaning?"

"Meaning somebody's desperate to use your death as an excuse to kill a treaty. Whether I think it's a good or bad treaty isn't relevant, Major. There's a man I work for who thinks it's a good treaty. And my job is to keep you alive." He walked across the room and stared out the window, but saw nothing out of the ordinary.

"Me, too," she commented from behind him.

He turned around and saw her standing near the couch, then glanced down and saw the small Beretta Jetfire automatic in her right hand. "Where did that come from?"

She smiled and pulled her robe open. "A chamois holster I wear inside my thigh." She looked at the four-inch-long weapon. "Small but effective."

Schwarz knew how deadly the Italian-made weapon could be at close range. "You've got dangerous thighs."

She snapped on the safety and laid the automatic down on an end table, then walked toward him. "Only to those who try to harm me."

He saw a new expression on her face. Gadgets wondered if it was admiration. Or was he kidding himself? "That's why I'm here. To make sure they don't." He couldn't understand why he felt a little nervous.

"As you saw, I can take care of myself."

He forced himself to sound tough. "So can the quarterback for the L.A. Rams, but I'll bet he's real grateful he's got all those other guys helping him out when he's facing a football field of big, mean pro players trying to beat his head into the dirt. If you understand football," he added.

"You mean American's imitation of Russian soccer? Of course I do." She smiled at him, daring him to top her comment.

He held his hands up in surrender.

"That was the only thing I found wrong with Cal Tech. No football," she added.

Gadgets escaped across the room to a small table where a stack of magazines were piled. He thumbed through them idly.

"Bored already?" she asked.

"No. But there doesn't seem like a lot we can talk about without giving away secrets or getting into an argument."

"You could start by telling me who you really are. Army majors who parade as specialists in nuclear arms do not conduct themselves like experts in guerrilla warfare," she said, needling him.

"Nor do Russians with doctorates," Gadgets retorted. He looked at her and waited for a reply. Instead, he saw her examining him carefully. For some reason he suddenly felt like a side of beef being inspected for its quality.

"I guess there is not much we can talk about without facing the hostility of our superiors," she agreed.

Gadgets nodded and looked down at the copy of *Time* magazine. He kept turning the pages without stopping to look at them.

Her voice became quieter and softer as she made a comment. "They did say it would take at least ninety minutes to deliver?"

He began to understand. His voice lost its edge as he replied, "At the soonest."

She stared at him. "Are you married?" she suddenly asked.

"Never had the pleasure," he replied. "Or the problem."

"Is there anything we could do that would not require our revealing professional secrets?"

Gadgets smiled as he thought of the only logical solution. "Yeah, I can think of one thing," he said.

She didn't have time to ask what that was as he took her hand and led her into one of the bedrooms.

15

The afternoon news shows carried live coverage of the second massacre of the day. Dozens of cameramen and interviewers converged on the police captain in charge of the investigation and bombarded him with questions.

Who were the dead men? Who where they after? Or was somebody after them?

He told them all the same thing. The FBI and police were still investigating.

Hollings snapped off the set and picked up the phone to call Mexico. At least, he reminded himself as he waited for the call to go through, no one was announcing a connection between the redheaded bitch and the amateurs that the stupid German had hired.

Finding the Russian major at the Pentagon had been a long shot, anyway. He should have used the Shiites. If she had been anywhere in that vast, ugly complex, they would have found her.

In all fairness to Wittsinger, he had recruited some good men for him in the past. And, Hollings reminded himself, it wasn't kind to speak poorly of the dead.

Ruiz came on the phone. Hollings reported what had happened without making apologies. Ruiz was equally emotionless. They were both professionals.

"What do you plan to do?"

"Get out to California and finish the mission," the ex-KGB officer said. Then he told the Mexican he'd contacted a man he had used before on a similar mission. Ibrahim Nidar. "He's costly," he warned.

"Are his men any good?"

"They're religious fanatics. Shiites."

"I don't know if you can count on men like that in a fight," Ruiz said, sounding doubtful.

"I've used them before. They don't turn and run." He told him about the last time. Ten years ago.

Ruiz seemed satisfied. "Get the money you need from the banker." He was quiet for a moment. "We've finally agreed on a replacement for him."

Hollings understood. He'd have to call Nidar and have him rig more explosives.

Hollings waited until dark, then called a cab and had it take him to Constitution Avenue and Seventeenth Street. Casually strolling down the crowded Mall, he glanced at the other pedestrians who passed under the streetlights. Most of them were families of tourists, daring the near-record summer heat to stare in admiration at the Washington and Lincoln Memorials.

Hollings paused to make sure nobody was tailing him. A pair of young blacks walked by, carrying a giant portable music system turned to a radio station specializing in heavy metal. He gritted his teeth. The sound had begun to invade the peaceful suburb of Mexico City where he lived.

As he wandered down one of the dark paths, he saw a small group of long-haired men and women sitting on the grass, listening to another man strumming a guitar and singing a sad song about the death of some Latin American patriot.

Hollings smiled to himself. He was familiar with the story. He should have been. It was he who had been hired to assassinate him. He now realized he hadn't charged Ruiz enough. But he had been young and naive about how much somebody was willing to pay for an assassination. He hadn't been that naive for a long time.

Mallincott was sitting on a bench, dressed in a custom-made English suit and shoes. He was trying to read the *Wall Street Journal* under a streetlamp.

Hollings checked to make sure no one showed any interest in him. A young girl with long stringy red hair was lying on the grass, her eyes closed. She lifted her head and glanced at him, then lowered it and closed her eyes.

As Hollings approached the bench, Mallincott looked up at him, then moved over and returned to reading his paper. Hollings sat down beside the man and turned his head away to stare at the church tower.

"My friend in California is expecting you," the banker said in a low voice.

"Anything else I should know?"

"None of my friends seem to have much information about the time of arrival of the Soviet team, or the departure time of the American group. All they know is that they'll all meet at Edwards before they go their individual ways." Mallincott turned to face the former Russian agent. He looked worried. "It must be happening soon. General Cassidy, who's coordinating the American end of the disarmament program, is leaving tonight from Andrews Air Force Base in Washington to fly there."

Hollings made a mental note to call the Arab. If his men could get to Cassidy and find the woman tonight, he might not have to make the long, exhausting trip to California.

Mallincott interrupted his thoughts. "Ruiz said you needed some money. How much?"

Hollings named a sum that was enough to cover Nidar's services and expenses. The elegantly dressed older man was about to say no, when he remembered that the quarterly meeting to review the bank's situation was coming up in a few weeks.

"Stop by the bank tomorrow morning," the Banker said, "on your way out of town. I'll have a briefcase ready for you." Mallincott stood up and carefully folded his newspaper.

Hollings watched him leave. Something about the man made him decide to find another place to stay tonight. He felt that the motel was no longer safe.

16

For almost an hour Gadgets and the Russian woman made love. Flirtation gave way to excitement, which in turn surrendered to impatience. Then the need to accelerate became urgent.

There was no awkwardness or embarrassment. It was as if they had known each other forever. Each sensed the other's need and pampered it without sacrificing their own pleasure.

For Gadgets it was as close to being complete with another person as he had ever been. Except that he sensed something was still missing. It wasn't distrust; it was something else and he thought he knew what.

Irina had come so close many times to overcoming that final barrier that prevented her from experiencing completeness. But each time she came to the edge of the cliff of her surrender she would quickly pull back. What he didn't know was why.

It wasn't her training or the life they both led. It was something from her past. He wanted to ask her what, but instinctively knew he shouldn't. She would tell him in her own time. And only if she wanted him to know.

Gadgets reached out to the nightstand and turned the small radio to an FM station playing jazz ballads. He stretched his hand out to touch hers.

Her eyes were closed, but as she felt his fingers touch her, she opened her hand and closed it on his. For ten minutes they lay next to each other, letting the air-conditioning dry their bodies. They said nothing. Several times he was tempted to speak but something changed his mind.

What had happened between them was magic. Sometimes magic came only once for two people. But every so often it did return to happen again. Gadgets liked that thought.

"Thinking about anything in particular?" Irina asked.

He turned his head and smiled at her. Her eyes were still closed. "Private thoughts," he replied. "How about you?"

"Private thoughts," she replied. "But very pleasant ones."

"I had hoped they would be even more pleasant." It was the closest he could come to asking her what was wrong.

"I came closer than I've come in many years." She turned her head and looked at him with affection. "You're very special."

"Would you put that in writing?" he teased.

She laughed as she sat up. "And get kicked out of my job for favoring the Americans?" She jumped off the bed and slipped on her robe. "I'll be right back. I wonder what happened to the pizza."

As she walked into the bathroom, he knew their time of intimacy had just run out. "It'll be here soon," he called as she closed the bathroom door.

Reluctantly Gadgets pulled on his jeans and shirts, then reached down and tucked the Colt automatic back inside his waistband. Unwilling to let go of the still-pleasurable sensations wandering through his body, he stretched and glanced at the disheveled bed that had brought him so much joy. But an insistent hammering at the front door cut short his romantic musing. The pizza delivery man had arrived.

The bathroom door opened. Looking fresh and radiant, the Russian woman emerged and smiled at him. "Do we split the bill, or am I the American government's guest for dinner?" she asked, reaching for the briefcase she had dropped on an end table.

Gadgets quickly pulled out a twenty. "I don't know about Uncle Sam, but I think you're worth buying dinner for," he said, bowing grandly.

He was about to expand on the statement when they heard a harsh, guttural voice on the other side shout, "Open this damn door or we'll kick it in!"

Gadgets pulled the 10 mm Colt from his waistband and glanced at Irina. She had grabbed the Walther P-5 from her briefcase and was moving to his side.

Schwarz gestured for her to back him up as he braced himself against the wall next to the thick wooden front door. She set her legs in a shooting stance and aimed the 9 mm automatic at the door.

The hammering from outside continued. "I guess they want us to do it the hard way," the harsh voice announced loudly from the other side of the door.

Gadgets unlocked the safety on his automatic and pointed at the crack between the door and wall, then reached across with the other hand and gently twisted the handle. The door was shoved inward as he moved back and snapped into the two-handed stance, spreading his legs to steady himself.

Two men in casual sports clothes grinned at him as they moved into the room, carrying two large boxes and a large brown paper bag. Pol glanced at the gun in Gadgets's hand. "I've heard of guys trying to beat the pizza delivery men out of their money," he teased.

The muscular blond man shrugged. "Some guys are just cheap, I guess."

Feeling a little foolish, Gadgets lowered the automatic and turned to the redhead, who hadn't relaxed her shooting stance. "It's okay, Major. These two characters are friendlies."

Still suspicious, she let the hand holding the Walther move slowly down to her side.

"Gentlemen," Schwarz said, nodding to her, "meet the government's special guest from Russia, Major Tolstoy."

Pol licked an imaginary speck of dust from the front of his patterned short-sleeved silk sport shirt and glanced at the perfect creases in his knife-edged gabardine slacks before he bowed. "My pleasure, *señorita*." He looked at her with admiration. "If I had known there were women like you in Russia, I would have defected a long time ago."

Gadgets winked at the Russian. "In our country we call that being slick."

"In ours we call it bullshit," she replied, shaking her head at Blancanales. "If that's the best you can do, you must be very lonely at night."

Lyons and Schwarz collapsed with laughter while Pol tried to pretend he hadn't heard the comment.

"First woman I heard who got your number right off the bat, Homes," Ironman cracked.

"Look who she's had for company," Pol retorted. "The genius probably fed her something to dull her good taste."

Irina stared at the burly blond man. He looked as if his muscles were trying to burst out of the cage of the gaudy sport shirt he was wearing over his unpressed jeans. She turned to Gadgets. "Would you introduce me, Major Schwarz?" she asked, then turned and looked at Pol. "I know how this one thinks, but not his name."

Politician shook his hand as if the Russian woman had burned it.

"The one with the werewolf fangs is Captain Rosario Blancanales," Schwarz told her.

Pol clicked his heels together, imitating a Hollywood version of a commissioned officer.

Gadgets nodded toward Lyons. "The other one is Captain Carl Lyons, who likes to throw his weight around when he isn't lifting them."

"Just for that," Ironman said, setting the two pizza boxes down on the dining table, "we won't invite you two to dinner."

"We planned to serve you a typical American feast, *señorita*," Pol added. "American pizza." He looked down at his clothes. "I trust you'll pardon the fact that we're not in uniform."

"If you don't mind my wearing this robe until after we eat," she replied with a smile that hinted at her interest in him.

"Forever, *señorita*, if you wish," Blancanales said grandly.

Gadgets showed his irritation at the word game between the two until he saw Ironman touch his shoulder gingerly and wince. "You go hunting today?" he asked.

"I guess you could say that."

"Catch something?" Gadgets asked, still staring at the shoulder.

"Just a scratch."

"Like the scratch on your leg last month?" Gadgets asked.

"Since when did you become my mother?" Ironman growled.

Pol shook his head. "Don't waste your time. The man is as stubborn as a bull."

"And you're full of it," Lyons snapped, annoyed at the amount of attention the other two were giving to his injury.

Schwarz was about to add a comment, then remembered something and stared at his two partners. "Have you two been hanging around outside for a long time?" he asked, not bothering to disguise the hard edge in his voice.

"Long enough to tap the phone and change your order and add beer to it," Pol replied, grinning.

Irina Tolstoy studied the two newcomers. "Did you enjoy what you heard?" she asked coldly.

"We were too busy making sure the area was secure to pay any attention," Ironman assured her.

She examined his expression carefully and seemed satisfied. "Thank you," she replied with a hint of gratitude.

"You're welcome," he said, then turned to Gadgets. "We hear you had some excitement when you left the Pentagon. Sorry we weren't there to help, but we were otherwise occupied.''

Schwarz glanced at Major Tolstoy. ''I had all the help I needed.'' He turned to Pol. ''What were you two up to?''

''Catching up with some dirtbags who had just kidnapped and killed a woman at Dulles Airport.'' He looked directly at the Russian officer as he added, ''A redheaded woman, Major.''

She turned to Gadgets. ''Now we know who they're after.''

''We can talk about that later,'' Lyons insisted, staring impatiently at the boxes on the dining table. ''Right now let's eat.''

''You haven't lived until you've eaten an American pizza,'' Pol bragged.

''I know people who didn't live after they'd eaten an American pizza,'' she replied with a twinkle in her eye as she walked to the table.

Blancanales turned to Schwarz. ''Hey, she bites back,'' he commented. ''I thought Russians had no sense of humor.''

''The major attended Cal Tech as a graduate student,'' Gadgets told him.

A flicker of surprise crossed Lyons's face, then he grinned as he said, ''If the Beach Boys had met the major back then, they could had added Russians to their song about California girls.''

Irina looked at him with a puzzled expression. ''Is that a compliment or an insult?''

''I wouldn't worry about it,'' Schwarz told her. Then he glanced at the pizza on the table and said, ''At least until after we eat.''

She looked at the two boxes. ''Why two?'' she asked Lyons.

''One for you and one for me,'' he answered.

''What about the other men?''

''I meant one for all of you,'' Lyons explained with a straight face.

"Ignore him, Major," Schwarz warned. "He's just a growing boy whose brain can't keep up with his body."

"That's better than being a brain without a body," Lyons snapped back.

"I know some women who would argue that my body isn't too damn bad," Gadgets bragged.

Irina lifted a wedge of deep dish pizza from the box. As she brought the gooey slice to her mouth, she commented, "You two can keep fighting while I eat."

"A woman after my own heart," Ironman said, grabbing a wedge from the other box.

"Hey, wait for me!" Gadgets yelled, racing Blancanales to the table.

POL TOOK A LAST SIP from the nearly empty beer bottle, burped softly and collapsed on the couch. "Excuse me," he said, dropping the empty bottle onto the rug.

"I think I've had it," Ironman admitted, flopping down next to him.

"Sure you're not still hungry?" Gadgets needled Lyons. "There's some chunks of cheese stuck to the sides of the boxes you could nibble at."

Lyons waved the offer away.

Schwarz turned to the Russian major. "Satisfied?"

She eased herself down on the rug, then stretched and smiled contentedly. "In every way."

Gadgets lowered himself to the rug next to her. "Ditto," he agreed in a quiet voice. He lifted his head and stared at Blancanales and Lyons. "How'd you two find us?"

"Can't the questions wait until I'm finished digesting?" Pol groaned.

"No," Gadgets said.

"The man gave us the address, Homes," Lyons replied.

"The man?" Irina asked.

"Our boss," Ironman replied without giving her Brognola's name or title.

"What is this word *Homes*?" she asked. Gadgets explained the term. She wrinkled her nose disdainfully. *"Nyet kultur,"* she commented in Russian.

"I don't need Russian lessons to know what that means," Pol said, looking at her. "So you don't think we have any class?"

"No," she replied, then put on an innocent face and stared into space. "But some of you have a lot of style."

Gadgets turned red and refused to acknowledge the glances he got from his two partners. He turned quickly to the Russian and tried to change the subject. "I forgot to ask you—" he started to say.

"Before you got too busy, Homes?" Pol asked, jumping in.

Ignoring him, Schwarz continued. "Did you know a Rich Levinson at Cal Tech, Major?"

Irina looked uncertain as she searched through her memory. Finally she turned to him and asked, "About your height with reddish hair?"

"That's the man," Gadgets said.

"Very quiet. Majored in engineering," she added, still focusing on her recollections. "Why?"

Schwarz's voice became solemn and quiet. "He was the pilot of the American transport that was sabotaged."

A heaviness suddenly descended over the group. Irina shook her head sadly. "I knew most of the men and women who died when our transport crashed."

Suddenly they were all reminded why they were there.

"It won't happen again," Gadgets said. The way he said it made his words sound more like a guarantee than a promise.

"You bet it won't," Lyons agreed. "We're getting out of here before it does."

"To go where?" Irina asked suspiciously.

"California," Lyons replied.

"My group doesn't arrive there for several days," she said.

"That's been changed," Pol told her. "Your people leave for Edwards tomorrow morning before anyone else gets a chance to play games with their transport plane."

"And your team?" she asked.

"They'll wait until your group gets here. Then, according to our boss, they'll spend some time exchanging suggestions about how they can better monitor the dismantling before our group leaves for Russia."

Gadgets jumped in. "Is that smart if somebody's out to stop them?"

"Boss says the DOD—" Lyons started saying, then turned to the Russian woman. "That's our Department of Defense."

"I know what the DOD is," she replied.

"The DOD has rented an entire motel near the base where the two teams will stay under military protection."

"What are we supposed to do?" Gadgets asked.

"What we do best," Lyons replied with a tight grin. He turned to the Russian major. "There's a military jet transport waiting at Andrews Air Force Base to take us there nonstop."

"And Cowboy packed us a couple of cases of treats to take with us in case we get hungry," Pol added.

Gadgets understood. Kissinger was sending along a selection of his personally modified weapons. Knowing how the resident armorer thought, Schwarz knew there would be enough variety to suit any situation that arose.

Major Tolstoy had been listening to the veiled comments between the three men with a glint in her eyes. "This does not sound," she observed, putting some bite into her words, "like the kind of conversation three military officers whose sole purpose in being here is to act as escorts would be having. It sounds more like three soldiers getting ready to go into battle."

"You know about the Boy Scouts, Major?" Ironman asked.

She nodded.

"We believe in their motto," he told her. "Be prepared."

"I get the impression the three of you are used to being prepared," she said.

"Let's talk about that another time," Pol said. "Why don't we get out of here before somebody else finds out where you're staying?"

"I should be ready in a few minutes. I just have to put on my uniform," she told them.

Pol and Ironman exchanged glances.

"Why don't you not do that?" Lyons suggested. "Just in case somebody out there has decided it's open season on redheaded Russian majors in uniform."

She thought about it. "Agreed. What do you suggest I wear?" she asked in the same tone of voice she might have asked a KGB weapons expert which handgun he recommended she carry on a specific mission.

"Ask your friend," he said, nodding at Gadgets. "He probably has a better idea of what you should and shouldn't wear than me."

Gadgets started to make a bitter comment, then caught himself. "Let's see if I've got anything you'd like to borrow," he said. Then he saw the questioning expressions on the other men's faces and added, "As a disguise."

As they entered his bedroom, the hard expression on her face vanished. She looked softer, sadder as she said, "I was hoping we wouldn't be leaving until morning."

"Me, too," he admitted quietly. "Hopefully there'll be another time."

A few minutes later she walked out of Gadgets's bedroom, carrying several items, and vanished into her own room. Gadgets followed her out five minutes later, lugging his briefcase and overnight bag. Without a word he dropped them onto the floor and walked to the closed door of the other bedroom.

"Need a hand?" he called out.

The door opened a crack in response to his question and he disappeared inside. Pol watched as the door closed again, then turned to Carl and shook his head. "It isn't often that I wish there was enough time for us to act like other people."

Lyons didn't hear him. He was staring out the large living room window. Pol understood what his partner was seeing in the moonlit night outside.

The face of a dead young woman he had loved.

17

There were a half-dozen cars parked in the paved area around the town house complex, but no people. At least nobody was visible.

Pol and Ironman opened the front door of the safe-house, holding their handguns ready to fire. They went out to the Dodge suburban van first to make sure nobody was waiting in ambush. Then they unlocked the doors and checked inside.

The two large metal cases were sitting on the floor in the rear, just as they had been when they had gone inside earlier. Next to them were Lyons's and Blancanales's hanging bags that contained their clothes and toilet kits.

Pol looked at the one-way side and rear windows that permitted them to look out but prevented anybody from seeing who was inside the van. They were ready to roll.

Lyons got behind the wheel and started the engine while Blancanales turned to the town house and whistled softly.

Gadgets came out, his Delta Elite cocked and tightly gripped. He helped a small figure wearing a baseball cap, T-shirt and jeans into the rear seats of the van. In one hand the figure carried a briefcase; in the other a Walther P-5.

Schwarz ran back to the house and grabbed several suitcases and his briefcase, then turned and rushed them to the vehicle. He tossed them into the rear and climbed inside.

"Ready?" Lyons asked as Gadgets slid the side door shut.

"Ready," he replied, then turned to the baseball-capped figure next to him. "How about you?"

For a moment there was no sound. Then a slim hand reached up and pulled off the cap. "Can I speak now?" Irina asked.

Lyons nodded.

"Then I am ready."

Gadgets stared at her with admiration.

The Russian major was wearing a T-shirt that was too large for her slim form. It was that special shade of Dodger Blue, and the slogan across it proclaimed she was a fan of the Los Angeles Dodgers. With the wrinkled blue jeans and German-made leather running shoes he had suggested she wear, Irina looked like the typical American woman. At least, Schwarz thought as he stared at her, the typical beautiful American woman.

She had pinned her hair up so that she could hide it under the baseball cap she'd borrowed from Gadgets. It hadn't totally hidden her glowing rust-colored tresses, but it had made them more difficult to see.

"If Tommy Lasorda could see you dressed like that," Gadgets, the eternal baseball fan, exclaimed enthusiastically, "he'd make the team knock in a couple of extra home runs in your honor."

"Unfortunately I do not think my superiors would be as appreciative as Lasorda," the Russian major replied, looking down at her disguise. She stared out through the window. "Do you think anybody was watching?"

As if to answer her question, there was a hammering at the driver's door. The three men grabbed for their weapons, then Ironman looked out of his side window. A military vehicle had pulled up. Two armed MPs got out and walked over to the van, gesturing for him to roll down his window.

Lyons glanced at his partners. They had their guns drawn and cocked. He looked at the woman. A Walther automatic had magically appeared in her right hand. He turned around and opened the window a crack. "Yeah, what is it?"

"We've got a passenger for you," one of them said.

"We don't take passengers," Lyons snapped.

A deep voice joined in. "You do now," it called out.

The newcomer was wearing the uniform of a general, complete with a pair of stars on the epaulets of his Eisenhower battle jacket. "I'm General Cassidy."

Ironman looked skeptical until he glanced at Gadgets, who was smiling at the new arrival. "Do you always hitch rides to the airport in the middle of the night, General?"

"Only when I get a chance to ride there next to a good-looking redhead," Cassidy replied.

Gadgets opened the side door and introduced the general to his two partners. Irina smiled quietly and held out her hand to the older man.

"I've got one of my own, thank you," he said, looking down at the Walther in her hand and patting his pocket.

She blushed slightly, slipped the automatic back inside her handbag and moved over to make room for him beside her.

"Why didn't you have your own people drive you to Andrews, General?" Pol asked, looking puzzled.

"I wanted to make sure I got there," Cassidy replied bluntly. He noticed the questioning expressions on all of their faces before he turned to Gadgets. "I got a chance to talk to your chief of operations."

"Any reason you think you wouldn't have made it without us?" Gadgets asked.

"Let's just say I trust my gut instincts." He glanced behind him at the three large cases. "What's in those boxes?"

"Some supplies," Lyons grunted.

Cassidy stared at Ironman's face reflected in the rearview mirror. "Nothing nuclear, I hope."

Lyons shrugged. "I don't know. But I wouldn't think so. We haven't used anything nuclear before."

"Well, I'm grateful for small mercies, Captain Lyons. But I suggest we get our asses in gear before someone we don't like figures out where we are."

Ironman put the vehicle in gear and sped out of the parking lot.

Gadgets glanced at the general. He had his eyes closed and seemed to be dozing. "You okay, General?" he whispered.

Cassidy opened his eyes. "Fine, as long as I've got this in my hand."

Schwarz looked down and saw the 9 mm Browning Hi-Power the general had wrapped his large hand around. "I got the impression you were a pacifist, General."

"A live pacifist," Cassidy replied. "And I intend to stay that way."

His comments were interrupted by the sound of squealing tires as Ironman twisted the steering wheel to avoid hitting the produce truck that was stalled on the road in front of them.

"What the hell is that?" Cassidy shouted.

Ironman swerved around the stalled truck and jammed his foot down on the accelerator. "I don't know," he shouted, "but it smells wrong!"

Pol and Gadgets jumped over the seats to the back of the van and threw open the rear door as the truck began to pursue them.

A pair of hands shoved what looked like a SIG Model 550 assault rifle out of the front passenger window and began to squeeze off rounds.

Lyons ran the van in a broken field pattern to avoid the barrage of armor-piercing slugs, while his two partners grabbed their handguns and poured lead at the pursuing vehicle's front windshield. Despite the hits they scored with every round, they knew that even the powerful .45-caliber round that Blancanales was firing would have little impact when fired from a relatively short-barreled handgun at that distance.

Suddenly the searing light of a 40 mm incendiary grenade exploded on the road between their van and the pursuers, momentarily blinding both of them. Before they could figure out what had happened, the barrel of a 12-gauge shotgun poked between them and began pumping a mixture of slugs and double O shot at the rooftop assassin. They barely heard the shriek of the swarthy-skinned man as lead burned into him and shoved his body onto the road.

Pol turned to see who had joined them. The face of the senior military officer was twisted in anger as he relentlessly continued to shove searing lead at the truck. "Nobody messes with a national treasure!" Cassidy shouted in fury as he paused to stare at the barely visible body on the ground.

Gadgets looked past him and saw Irina kneeling over the metal cases. She had opened the covers and was handing the senior officer shotgun shells. She then grabbed several fragmentation grenades and joined in the battle.

Schwarz pulled a fully loaded Galil assault rifle from the case and tossed it to Pol. All three of the Able Team hell fighters regarded the Israeli-made weapon as one of the most reliable available to military forces. He chose an AR-15 Delta Elite H-Bar sniper rifle and shoved in a magazine loaded with the awesome rounds.

Quickly pocketing three extra magazines, Schwarz joined the others in the rear while Ironman concentrated on second-guessing the attackers as to where they would place their shots next.

"At the engine!" Gadgets shouted at Blancanales, who responded by focusing his fire at the front grille.

The general kept pouring shot at the rooftop, hoping to dissuade anyone else from climbing onto it. Schwarz focused his firepower on the front windshield, pouring round after round at the safety glass.

Irina sat up, and before Gadgets could pull her down out of the possible path of a ricocheting slug, pulled the pin on a grenade and carefully rolled it into the path of the oncoming vehicle. The earsplitting sound waves of lead fragments tearing through the floor of the truck mingled with screams of pain from the driver as the vehicle swerved off the road into a ditch, then ran up a slight incline and stopped dead.

"That should take care of the bastards," Cassidy cursed, relaxing the tense grip on the shotgun stock.

"Not yet," Irina snapped as she pulled the pin on the second grenade and tossed it at the four men who poured out of the rear of the truck. They were firing their AK-47s on full autoburn. Bits of flesh and blood sprayed across the side of the truck as two of the attackers disintegrated.

Ironman stomped on the brakes. Gadgets and Pol jumped from the van and charged at the truck as three assailants jumped out of a side door of the vehicle. They were firing their Uzis and screaming oaths in a foreign language.

"I've got the ones on the right," Gadgets shouted and, without waiting for Blancanales's acknowledgment, carefully placed three shots, then watched as the trio he had hit suddenly stopped and crumbled to the ground. Three shots, three hits, three kills.

Pol squeezed off two rounds and saw the pair he had hit spin wildly, then fly backward as their bodies were torn apart by his armor-piercing rounds.

The driver's door opened and a small wild-eyed man jumped out, waving an AK-47 at them. Before either of the two could fire, they heard the authoritative impact of two hollowpoints and watched him fold in half.

Lyons had joined them. He looked around at the carnage. "That should end their game," he said in satisfaction.

They heard another shot being fired on the far side of the truck. They turned and saw Irina standing at the opened driver's door, smoke curling from the muzzle of her Walther. She reached a hand inside and dragged out the body of a thin woman, still gripping a 40 mm fragmentation grenade in her clenched fist. Carefully freeing the grenade from the dead woman's grasp, she let the shattered body fall onto the road, then looked at the men and coldly commented, "Now it does."

FOLLOWING THE DIRECTIONS given them by the guards at the number three entrance to Andrews Air Force Base, Ironman drove the van past a large parked luxury jetliner with the words Air Force One painted in bold letters on the side.

Irina stared with admiration at the plane. "That's the private plane of your President, is it not?"

It was the first words any of them had spoken since the ambush, and Gadgets smiled at her expression. "Pretty nice perk, isn't it?"

She looked puzzled. "Perk? Like in making coffee?"

"You haven't been here for a long time, have you?" Pol asked.

She shook her head.

"The word *perk* means an extra bonus that goes with the job," Gadgets jumped in to explain.

"You think that's what they're flying us out on?" Pol asked, unsuccessfully trying to look naive.

"You'd die of boredom with all the fancy food and booze they'd force you to eat," Gadgets needled.

"I'm ready for a little boredom after tonight," Blancanales cracked.

"Aren't we all," Gadgets agreed.

Lyons said very little as he continued to follow the route the armed guard at the gate had given him until the van came to a remote section of the base where a long, sleek military jet was parked. "This is it, Homes. More our style," he told Blancanales, forcing himself to sound relaxed.

Gadgets and Pol looked at him as he tried to hide his attempt to work the pain out of his shoulder by exercising it gently. Pol turned away from him and stared at the 150-foot-long military aircraft. He had never seen anything quite like it. It had 145 feet of wingspan, four huge Pratt and Whitney turbojets suspended under the swept-back wings and an unusual superstructure mounted high above the middle of the craft.

Three jeeps suddenly appeared, racing at them from different directions. Inside each were four armed soldiers. "You got any reason for being here?" the one whose shoulders carried the insignia of a major asked brusquely, sticking his head into the van and staring at the four passengers.

Ironman handed him a set of official-looking documents. The major scanned them carefully, then looked inside the van again. "Who's Major Schwarz?" he demanded.

"I am," Gadgets replied, gripping his automatic tightly. He could sense the others had their weapons ready, too, just in case the officer turned out to be one of the enemy.

"I'm Major Frehling with base security," the officer said, relaxing. He turned and gestured to the armed men in the military vehicles to lower their assault rifles, then turned and looked at Lyons. "If you'll pull this van up to the rear cargo door, my men will help you load your luggage."

As Ironman moved the van slowly onto the hard-faced field and alongside the long silver jet, Pol said, "Now that's the way to travel."

"The VIP version of the Lockheed C-140B, I believe," the Russian major answered automatically, then realized the four men in the van were staring at her.

"You know an awful lot about our jets," Ironman commented.

"A good Russian knows a lot about a lot of things," she said coyly.

"Especially a good Russian agent," Gadgets replied bluntly.

She said nothing as she got out of the van and entered the huge military jet. Neither did any of the men of Able Team as they watched the soldiers carry their two metal boxes aboard.

As THE PLANE PUSHED its way through the upper atmosphere toward California, Irina tried to start a conversation. None of the four men seemed interested in talking. Not even Major Schwarz whom she sat next to.

Lyons kept tossing in his seat, then finally got up and returned with a paper cup filled with water. He fished two vials out of his pocket, took a pill from each and swallowed them, washing them down as the other two men watched him but said nothing.

Cassidy turned to Gadgets. "That was impressive the way you wiped out those bastards back there on the road. I guess your work when you aren't protecting foreigners prepared you for such an ambush."

Lyons's irritation at having their identity revealed, even by someone with the top-security clearance of General Cassidy, showed on his face. He didn't like outsiders to know who they were. Even the most discreet official couldn't be trusted to keep his mouth shut all the time.

Irina made Cassidy's comments seem small-time with her next comment. "You mean about them being part of the commando group called Able Team?" she asked with an air of innocence.

Cassidy looked at the stunned expressions on the faces of the three men and laughed. "Something like that," he admitted.

"What do you know about Able Team?" Gadgets asked, raising his guard again.

"Very little. Some of our people hate you. But so do a great many drug distributors and common criminals from what we hear. You are reputed to be excellent commandos and expert with many different kinds of weapons." Her eyes sparkled as she added, "I can personally vouch for the last two facts."

"And you, Major, are with the KGB," the general replied.

It was her turn to look surprised. Quickly she masked the expression. "Why do you say that, General?"

"Aside from common sense? Well, your tuition at Cal Tech was paid for by an international pacifist organization that has since been found to have close ties to the KGB," he said. "And you're not dull enough to just be a scientist."

"Very strange logic," she protested. Her face suddenly showed her concern. "Does this mean you will force me to return home?"

"Hell, no!" Cassidy said in a loud voice that startled the others. "What it means is that you're prohibited from visiting your alma mater since they're doing some very confidential development work for the DOE and for us."

"Much of which we are already aware of," she replied, trying to regain her balance.

"You should be aware that we plan to keep an eye on you to make sure you don't see anything you're not supposed to see. If those terms are acceptable, Major, then I think we can continue as we were."

She pursed her lips and weighed the offer. "Agreed," she said, then looked at the other three men. "If that is agreeable with them."

Pol shrugged. "Almost anything is agreeable when a beautiful *señorita* is involved."

Lyons returned to his seat and showed his unhappiness. "Sounds risky to me." He looked at Schwarz. "But if the science whiz over there promises to keep a constant eye on her, I guess I can go along with you," he conceded.

The Russian turned and looked at Schwarz. He looked back at her, studying her face and eyes. "If it's okay with the major, I'm willing," he said, trying to make it sound impersonal.

"It is acceptable," she replied coyly.

Cassidy looked at Schwarz and then at Irina. Suddenly he broke into a loud laugh. "Talk about masking your feelings. You two could give lessons!" He got up and vanished into the cockpit.

"Do you think there will be trouble?" she asked Schwarz.

"Probably," he replied casually, and closed his eyes.

The general returned and sat down, looking less restless. One by one the men curled up in their seats, closed their eyes and dozed off.

She envied them their ability to so easily let go of whatever was on their minds and fall asleep. Even after all these years she couldn't. Finally, after tossing and turning for a half hour, she did.

She woke up once and glanced out the window at the blackness below, then realized her head had been resting against Major Schwarz's shoulder. She glanced at him and wondered if he knew she was there.

His face was quiet and calm, empty of the energy and animation she had seen in it when they had been fighting side by side. And later when they were making love.

She felt a sense of loss, this time more than ever before. It was a feeling she rarely ever experienced anymore.

Probably just as well, she reminded herself. She was here to get a job done and not to get involved in a romance that could go nowhere.

It was a rotten world sometimes, she decided as she moved closer to the Able Team warrior and fell asleep again with her head on his shoulder.

18

The unplanned meeting had run late into the evening, but the call from the Pentagon notifying the base commander to expect both the Russian and American teams several days earlier than originally planned had put extra demands on everybody at Edwards Air Force Base. Especially General Michael Halloran and his team.

By the time the rest of the top brass at Edwards were aware of the change in plans, Halloran had already been notified and asked to provide security for the two teams. And for the two nuclear missiles they were shipping to Edwards. Halloran made a mental note to call Mallincott and make sure this new information was passed along to the right people.

Nobody at Edwards knew what Halloran and his people did aside from providing security services. That was the way the Intelligence Coordinating Board operating out of the White House wanted it. However, it was obvious they were more than military cops.

Most of the unexplained flights that arrived at and departed from Edwards fell under Halloran's supervision. So did the groups of unidentified people who frequently showed up at the base and were almost immediately rushed onto a plane and flown away by one of his special crews.

He looked around the large table in the conference room next to his office. The eight men sitting there looked exhausted. He gathered up the papers in front of him and shoved them into a folder stamped Top Security, then glanced at the others. "Anyone have anything to add?" he asked.

They all shook their heads and pushed their papers into similar folders.

"Then I suggest we get some sleep," he announced. Turning to the bald officer on his right, he added, "Except for you and me, Jack. We stay up and greet the first arrivals before we hit the sack."

Halloran waited until only the two of them were in the conference room. "Did we hear from the other man yet?"

"Nothing yet. He's supposed to call when he gets in."

Halloran pulled himself to his feet. "Call me when the tower announces that the Lockheed from Andrews is on its final approach. I'll be in my office."

He opened the door to his large, darkened office and glanced out the window behind his desk. He could almost see the desert on which Edwards Air Force Base had been built. Suddenly feeling older than his fifty-five years, the general locked the door behind him and stripped off his medal-heavy uniform jacket. Dropping it onto one of the coatrack hooks near the door, he gazed around the room.

A lifetime of defending his country against all enemies was represented by the photographs, certificates and awards mounted on the walls. His history of service was profiled within the frames—beginning with the day he'd graduated from the Air Force Academy, his time in Korea and then Vietnam, to his current stateside post as head of military security operations for the western half of the United States.

He'd met them all. Presidents, prime ministers, generals, admirals. Even dictators, he remembered with a sour expression as he glanced at the photograph of the now-dead Caribbean dictator who used a combination of voodoo and brutality to stay in power.

He'd spent a lifetime making certain that no one could deliberately or foolishly betray the country for selfish or supposedly noble reasons.

As he lowered himself into the chair behind his desk, he thought about the price he had paid for that decision. Passed over for promotions, and ridiculed by the press for speeches he had made about elected officials who were giving the country away to the Commies. All of that in a country for which he had fought so hard, for so long, to keep free.

He glanced at the framed photograph on his desk of an attractive young woman in her early twenties. Marcy was the one person who would have understood how he felt. But she wasn't here. The Russians had sent hired terrorists to kill her in the Beirut consulate office where she had been working on her first State Department assignment.

It still felt like yesterday. What he had done in the past few weeks was for her as well as for the country.

He turned his chair around and stared out the window into the darkness. In the distance he could see runway lights glowing like the birthday candles he still remembered burning on Marcy's cake when she was sixteen years old.

He'd wanted to back out a dozen times since the night Johnson had introduced him to the banker. They had both sold him on helping to save the country from the Commies.

But he hadn't. He stared out of the window in his office, looking for some sign that he had done the right thing. But all he could see was Marcy's smile, and that young major's last snappy salute before he climbed aboard the transport for his final mission.

Before he could either doze or dwell on it he heard a knock at his door and sat up. Colonel Jack Zearns walked in.

"They're coming in now," he announced. "Feel like joining the official greeting party?"

Halloran didn't want to see anybody right now. "Not if you can handle it alone," he said. "Where do you plan to put them?"

"At that apartment motel down the road from the base that we sometimes use for visiting VIPs. The Mojave View.

We rented the whole place so we could put up our own people and the Commies.''

Zearns started to leave, then stopped at the door and turned to look at the uniformed man behind the desk. ''I hope this is the end of it, Mick. You know I'm with you all the way, but this business of killing our own men...'' He left the rest of his speech unsaid as he walked out of the office.

Halloran waited until the colonel closed the door behind him, then leaned his head back and closed his eyes. The only good thing about all of this was that the nightmare would be over in a few days.

Except in his memory.

RICHIE LAMANTIA RAN a small gun shop on one corner of his six-acre Mojave Desert industrial site, located on the outskirts of the town of Mojave. Tucked into a small pocket near the Red River Canyon, the shop sold a wide variety of weapons to customers who were qualified to buy them. He even had a small outdoor range behind the shop that faced onto a garbage-filled arroyo.

But Richie was better known as a surplus dealer. Scattered on the rest of the lot were all types of used military trucks, vans and cars—even Korean War-Vintage tanks that didn't work. The tanks were often wanted by war buffs or film studios looking for cheap equipment they could use in war movies.

There wasn't much the tall fat man wasn't willing to offer good, hard cash for, especially when the seller was the military. Tents, uniforms, paratrooper boots, field cooking gear—the list was endless.

To look at him, it was hard to believe he had enough money to buy himself a decent meal. Typically he wore oversize unwashed jeans and a dirty, torn, long-sleeved flannel shirt—even on the hottest days. Shaving was an occasional event, so his face was always covered with a thick layer of dark, stubby hair. Only the fat Cuban cigar he always seemed to have in his mouth suggested he was richer than he appeared.

Richie Lamantia was a wealthy man, but he didn't believe in displaying it. He could demand better prices if his customers thought he was having a hard time making ends meet.

His property, located on a dead-end dirt road, was surrounded by a high wire mesh fence that kept out the vandals and bums who tried to steal things so that they could finance their next bottle of cheap wine.

If the high fence or one of his men didn't stop them, one of his two rottweilers would. The massive black canines had been trained by the police to attack. But each had proved to be unreliable. They wouldn't stop after cornering a suspect, but kept attacking until their victims were dead.

Richie had paid the vet who was supposed to put the vicious animals to sleep to sell them to him instead. Now, after more than a year of patient training, he had actually gotten the animals to obey his commands. That was essential to Richie. He didn't want to lose the men who worked for him, especially those who were allowed to enter the security area within the large factory building.

Lamantia stored his more valuable surplus inventory inside the onetime paint factory. Rolls of fake Persian rugs, large stocks of television sets and personal computers acquired at bankruptcy auctions, cases of auto parts, canned food and a hundred other items were stacked in tall rows set far enough apart to allow a forklift to move between them.

His most valuable inventory was stored beside his office in a steel-reinforced concrete room built right in the middle of the factory. One of the huge rottweilers spent all of his time inside the secured enclosure. Only a handful of his most trusted employees—those the massive rogue police dog had been trained not to attack—were permitted to enter the room. And even they could only go inside for only three reasons: to feed the dog, to clean up its mess or to move inventory in and out.

That was where the smartass he had hired several days ago had made his mistake last night. He'd hidden until everybody but the two night guards and the dogs had left, then picked the lock on the sliding door that was the only entrance to the room.

Lamantia heard about it from the guards when he came in this morning. Nobody had to tell him what had happened. The sickening smell of blood permeated the air inside the warehouse.

Richie and one of his lieutenants, Pete-O, peeked inside and saw the red stains on the massive animal's jaw. And the torn, still-bleeding carcass lying on the floor next to him. Lamantia quickly slid the door shut.

"What do you want us to do?" Pete-O asked him, still shuddering at what he had seen.

"Take Harry or one of the other guys and grab a couple of plastic bags and some shovels," he replied. "Scoop up the mess and bury it outside in the desert where we dumped the others."

Looking as if he was on the verge of throwing up, the other man shivered and walked away.

"And use some of that surplus hospital deodorant around the place!" he yelled after him.

Lamantia didn't know if the dead man had been an undercover cop or how much he had seen before the dog had torn him apart, but it didn't matter any longer. Who was he going to tell that he had discovered row after row of illegal weapons and their ammo?

If he'd gotten away, he could have reported that he had found a vast storehouse of handguns, assault rifles, machine guns, rocket and grenade launchers, remote detonation devices, machetes, bayonets and knives. Some of the weapons dated back to before the Second World War. But most had been manufactured more recently.

Lamantia didn't just carry American weapons. He carried guns from almost every country in the world. And enough ammunition to supply a small army, including an

L.A. street gang with several hundred members willing to pay top dollar for his wares.

Most of the inventory in the locked room came from employees of weapons manufacturing plants or military storage depots who needed to make some extra cash. Even rogue cops tried to earn some side money by selling weapons they had confiscated from the street gangs.

The list of sources were long. And they had one thing in common: they knew Richie Lamantia was always willing to make an offer on what they brought to him. His customers also knew he could provide them with almost any weapon they requested. He rarely struck out on filling requests. And even then it wasn't for not trying.

The last time was when some skinhead gang leader from Beverly Hills had wanted him to get hold of a nuclear missile, as if one were just lying around waiting to be stolen. Lamantia still laughed when he remembered the conversation with the strange kid.

"I was told you could supply any weapon for a price," the kid had complained.

"Hey, from what I found out these things are thirty-five feet long and weigh over ten thousand pounds. You need specially built two-ton flatbed trucks just to haul a couple of them around."

"I'm still interested in one," the kid had said.

Richie had thought he'd thrown him the knockout punch when he'd talked about price. "Uncle Sam spent over eight million bucks to make each one of them. If—I only said if—one was offered to me, I'd have to get…" He'd thought about what would shake the kid up. "I'd have to get about twelve million bucks."

"Would that include the warhead?"

Richie had had a hard time believing it. The kid had sounded serious.

"Yeah, but let's talk about that when and if one gets offered to me. And you provide the transportation if you want to move it out of the area."

He'd thought about taking in twelve million on one day for a long time. Even after he'd paid off whoever stole it, he could see himself raking in five or six million bucks.

Richie knew that most of his customers were pretty weird. For some of them guns were a necessary part of their business. Like the gangs and the drug dealers. For others guns were an obsession he satisfied from his secret inventory.

Personally Lamantia hated the things. He kept one—a .45 Colt Commander automatic so badly in need of reblueing that it wasn't salable—in the center drawer of his desk, but only for those times when a customer had the nerve to try to threaten him.

The rest of his guns represented money. A lot of money.

Like the amount he expected to collect later in the day from the caller with the Southern accent who had contacted him from the East earlier. He had placed an order he wanted to pick up this afternoon.

He had done business with the guy before. He never knew what the man wanted to use the guns for; Richie didn't care. Once the weapon was out of his hands, he forgot about it.

He picked up the two sheets of ruled yellow paper on which he had written the list of items the customer wanted. Combat knives, 40 mm incendiary and fragmentation grenades, assault rifles that could be set on full automatic, .45 and 9 mm automatic pistols, sound suppressors and three thousand rounds of ammunition for the various weapons.

He was mildly curious why the caller wanted the next group of items—U.S. Special Forces uniforms, combat boots and helmets, walkie-talkies, several surplus jeeps and a surplus Army van, all with government license plates.

As he checked the list against his current inventory, he punched the buttons on his desk calculator, circling those items he didn't have in stock or couldn't get his hands on quickly. Finally he came to the end and hit the Total button.

"Shit," he whistled as he read the amount he was going to collect. A rare smile of joy crept across his face. "This guy must be getting ready for the start of Word War III!"

He got up and opened the door of his office. "Harry and Pete, when you're done getting rid of that stiff, get your asses in here fast," he yelled. "We got us one hell of an order to fill!"

19

The two well-dressed men who boarded the first-class section of the 10:00 a.m. flight from Washington to Los Angeles weren't happy. If anyone had studied their faces closely, they would have seen the fatigue and disappointment in them.

The handsome olive-skinned man also looked frustrated. Ibrahim Nidar wasn't used to failing. It made him angry.

Nidar's people had found the American general—and the woman—last night. But they had also found that both were protected by a wall of firepower that couldn't be penetrated. They had all died in the ensuing battle except for the observer he had sent along in a small car to make sure his orders were carried out.

The report was confusing. His man wasn't sure who had done the shooting. At one point he claimed he saw the Russian woman, the general and their three bodyguards firing weapons.

Nidar had him killed.

Now the general and the woman were in California. Probably at Edwards Air Force Base. Probably still being protected by the bodyguards the observer had kept swearing were with them even as he'd died.

At least, Nidar consoled himself, he knew where the Russian woman was.

As they slid into their seats, Hollings turned to the Arab. "Did you make arrangements to have someone meet us in L.A.?"

"The entire group. I'm hoping we can be done with the business in twenty-four hours. Our foreign minister is speaking before the United Nations the day after tomorrow, and we're all expected to attend," he replied quietly.

Nidar glanced down at the leather attaché case he had slid under the seat in front of him. It was filled with the large down payment for his services. There was more than enough to give each of his men a little, pay for the merchandise he had ordered and still have a substantial amount left to pay for his own costly recreation.

He looked at the man sitting next to him. Hollings had closed his eyes. Speaking softly in the English accent he'd acquired at Cambridge, he said, "Is there anything else I should know?"

Without opening his eyes, Hollings replied, "If there is, y'all will find out after we get there."

The Arab diplomat smiled. He couldn't get over the other man's accent. If he hadn't known better, he would have sworn Hollings had been born and raised in an American community in the Deep South instead of in the small Soviet city of Kagul near the Romanian border.

He knew better than to push the former intelligence agent for information. He would release it when he was ready.

Nidar looked out of his window at the hot, bright sunlight, then pulled down the shade, closed his eyes and dreamed of all the pleasure his reward would buy him.

As the pilot waited for his turn to take off, the former KGB officer glanced over at his companion. Finally he had dozed off. Hollings was grateful. He had wanted to catch up on his sleep during the flight. But the constant interruptions from Nidar had made it impossible.

So did the glare from the picture being projected on the cabin screen to entertain passengers while they waited. A female reporter from the local television station was at the scene of some accident.

Hollings found headphones in the seat pocket in front of him and plugged them in. As he slipped them over his head, he heard the woman talking rapidly.

"Police aren't sure just what caused the car to explode. The only thing they know for certain is that Peter Mallincott, a prominent local banker and philanthropist, was killed in the explosion...."

The ex-intelligence officer removed the headphones and smiled as he leaned his head back. He wouldn't waste his time reveling in his success. There were still details to work out for the mission.

As before, the primary goal was for him not to get killed. Especially not now when he had acquired almost enough money to escape from the hideous profession.

For Ruiz, the goal was much simpler: make the implementation of the new treaty impossible for a long time. The simplest way to achieve that was to have classified documents found on the Russian major's body so that the Americans would believe her real purpose in being here was to steal their secrets, and for the Kremlin to denounce the incident as an attempt to make them look bad before the rest of the world.

It would mean he had to forgo the pleasure of finishing what the Russian woman had so painfully interrupted years ago when she had mistaken his advances. It would also mean finding the right person to credit with her death.

The military officer who had been assigned to escort her during her visit would have been the ideal candidate. But Wittsinger's people had spoiled that idea when they'd messed up the job. All they had needed to do was kill the two of them, then plant the documents on her and place the gun in his hand. Police logic would have pulled the pieces together and accomplished the desired results.

Now he had to find a new hero. But who? He thought about it for a long time, then realized he had a ready-made one available in California.

Halloran. The general was a patriot who didn't hide his hate for anything or anyone Russian. He would make a perfect hero.

There was one last thing he had to do. He had to find out where Tolstoy was staying. He thought about it, then smiled when the obvious solution came to him. He'd let her come to him.

She had warned him she would find and kill him someday, no matter how long it might take. Now she would have her chance. Once he knew what housing arrangements had been made for the Russian team, he'd make himself visible and let her track him down.

Then, with the help of Nidar's people, he could complete the mission. Satisfied that he had forgotten nothing, Hollings closed his eyes and let sleep overcome him.

GADGETS DRAGGED himself into his military uniform, shoved his 10 mm Colt automatic into his waistband and got himself down the stairs to the living room of the boringly furnished two-bedroom motel apartment. Pol, already wearing his captain's uniform, was leaning over Ironman, replacing the gauze pad that covered his shoulder wound. There was a telltale bulge under Blancanales's jacket where he wore his .45 Colt Government automatic.

Lyons had his khaki shirt off and was staring stoically at the framed monochrome print of the desert hanging on the far wall of the room.

Schwarz glanced at the wound. It had crusted and there was no indication of infection. It was typical of Carl Lyons to refuse to admit to himself that his shoulder wasn't yet fully healed for fear he would be forced to watch from the sidelines as his two partners continued to carry out the assignment.

Gadgets and Pol had talked about how they could help the hell-raiser they called Ironman give his body more time to heal and had agreed that anything they did along those lines would only push him into exerting even more of his still-limited energy. They admitted to each other that they had similar reactions when the battle-drained body had been theirs.

The only way to deal with a "brother in blood" as they had nicknamed each other, was not to do anything different.

Pol pressed the pad down to cover the wound. Lyons winced, then quickly forced a placid expression on his face as he held a telephone receiver to his ear. Schwarz didn't have to wonder for very long who was on the other end.

"I knew you'd remember who he was sooner or later. Thanks for the call, Bear. And tell Cowboy thanks for the boxes of goodies he packed for us." As he hung up, Lyons glanced at the metal boxes stacked against a wall in the front hall of the apartment they had slept in last night.

"Well?" Gadgets asked.

Pol had finished taping the pad to Lyons's shoulder.

"Well, what?" Ironman asked as he put his sport shirt back on.

"Who was the guy?"

Lyons looked puzzled, then remembered. "Oh, the one Bear called about. Well, he kept searching through the files of the various agencies and ran across an old report from the CIA station in Ankara, Turkey, complete with descriptions."

Pol and Gadgets were getting impatient. "For God's sake, what did it say?" Blancanales asked.

"Seems that a KGB agent defected ten years ago, and we have him. At least we had him until he got killed in a plane crash over Libya a year later while he was on a contract mission for the CIA."

"And he's miraculously come back to life," Pol commented coldly.

"You saw the composite Bear put together," Ironman said. He looked up at the other two men as he pulled on his shirt and stood up, tucking the tail inside his khaki officer's pants. As always, he was wearing the .357 Colt Python over his right rear pocket in a rigid leather holster.

Gadgets closed his eyes as if he was suddenly meditating. When he opened them again, he looked at Lyons and asked, "Who was the . . . ?"

Lyons interrupted. "Bear's miles ahead of you. The chief of station in Ankara at the time was a man named Martin Johnson, who was moved to Langley four years ago to head up a special group."

Pol's voice had an angry undertone as he asked, "Why doesn't somebody have a little talk with this Johnson and find out how a dead man can come back to life?"

"According to Bear, you'd have to wait until Johnson found a way to resurrect himself," Ironman said. "Somebody took a dislike to the man and iced both Johnson and his wife the day before yesterday."

"Which leaves us with more questions than we had before Bear called," Gadgets commented. "What was the ex-KGB creep's name?"

"Lubankov," a voice said coldly from the staircase.

The three men turned and saw Irina Tolstoy standing in the open door, dressed in the slate-blue uniform of a Russian major. Her red hair was pulled back behind her head and held primly in place with a large, plain barrette.

"You didn't lock your front door fully," she added in a flat voice.

Her eyes were expressionless as she walked over and took the composite from Ironman's hands. Gadgets detected the hate in her eyes as she studied it carefully without further comment.

"He was using the name Hollings last time anybody asked him," Lyons told her. "You know him?"

"Too well," the redhead said, handing the composite back.

"Care to share the information?" Gadgets asked.

"He's a psychopath and an expert at killing and sabotage. He has no loyalties and no feelings about anything or anyone. The reason he defected was that the Soviet authorities had issued a warrant for his arrest and probably execution for crimes committed against the state." She looked grim and controlled as she started to walk back up the stairs, then stopped to look at the three men. "He is also a sexual deviant who likes to rape and then murder young women."

Ironman whistled. "Sounds like a sweetheart. Who would hire a psycho like that?"

"Don't fool yourself. He's exceptionally qualified in killing. And he has contacts with many criminal groups around the world who are available for hire."

"Is that what he did with the KGB?" Gadgets asked.

"He went far beyond his orders most of the time. It was only because he managed to complete his assignments that he wasn't dismissed prior to his defection."

"What were his orders this time, Major? Killing innocent people, like my friend Rich Levinson?" Gadgets snapped.

"Ask the persons who hired him. Many of the people who died when the Antonov crashed were also innocent scientists," she retorted bitterly, and stared back at him.

The sudden sound of knocking at the front door startled the four, breaking the tension that was building in the room. Major Tolstoy recovered first. She glared at the three men. "So, since we do not trust one another, perhaps we should complete out assignments separately?" She looked at Gadgets. "As you know, I do not need a bodyguard."

"Anybody going to open the door?" a man's voice asked loudly.

Gadgets backed off. "Maybe I blew my cork at the wrong person, Major Tolstoy," he conceded sheepishly. "If I took it out on these two characters, they'd slug me."

"If you had continued, so would have I," she said, allowing the hint of a smile to appear on her face.

Pol went to the front hallway and opened the door. General Cassidy walked past Blancanales and stared into the living room. Even wearing a fresh uniform with the two silver stars that told the world he was a major general, Cassidy looked casually dressed and relaxed. From the smile he wore no one could guess that last night he had killed an enemy and cursed that the others had beat him to the rest of the ambushers. He studied the faces of the four people and shook his head. "If the expression on the face of the major is any indication, maybe we should hang on to our Pershing missiles for a while."

Gadgets grinned at the familiar figure. "We just started calling a truce when you rang the doorbell, General."

"At least we were discussing terms," Irina added softly.

"Good," the tall uniformed man replied.

Gadgets could feel his face getting redder as the general grinned at him, then turned to the other two men. "Anybody think of brewing any coffee? I haven't had my first cup yet and I'm a nasty bastard until I do."

Pol raised a hand. "Coming right up, General." He looked around the room. "You're not the only one."

"Glad to hear that," Cassidy replied, and watched Blancanales disappear into the kitchen. "Looks like we're the only people staying here. According to the manager, the government rented the whole place for the next forty-eight hours." He looked around the living room and saw the metal boxes on the floor. "I never got a chance to see what other little goodies you have in there."

"Just some more arms in case we need them," Gadgets replied, deliberately being vague.

"There seemed to be more than just 'some,'" Irina said.

Schwarz looked up at her, ready to snap a reply when the general spoke up. "Mind if I have a look?"

Gadgets looked at Lyons, who weighed the request, then nodded. Schwarz knelt and opened the first case while Cassidy and the Russian woman stood over him and watched.

Set inside the large, foam-lined metal box was an array of powerful assault weapons. A sawed-off 12-gauge shotgun fitted with a pistol stock, a 12-gauge Mossberg slug gun, two M-16s with night scopes mounted on them, an H&K-53 submachine gun, two mini-Uzi machine pistols rechambered to fire .45 ACP rounds, the .308 Galil assault rifle and the AR-15 Delta Elite H-Bar, chambered to handle 5.56 rounds. There were also a large number of fully loaded magazines that fitted the various weapons.

Cassidy stared at the assortment for a moment, then reached down and picked up one of the shotguns. "I seem to remember that this one had my initials on the trigger," he said, fondling it for a moment before putting it back. He stared at Schwarz. "What the hell's in the other case? A couple of tanks?"

"Not quite," Gadgets replied as he opened the second box and looked inside. There were a pair of modified Colt Government .45 ACP automatics and three of the Beretta 92-F 9 mm parabellum autos, with 15-round staggered magazines, that had become the standard side arm issue for the U.S. government.

In addition there was a variety of ammunition, as well as ten incendiary, fragmentation and CS hand grenades. And a first-aid kit. Schwarz wasn't surprised when he saw it; it was a necessity in their line of work.

"Just some side arms and a lot of nourishment for the items in the first case," Schwarz added calmly.

He looked up at the Russian. She looked impressed.

"You're welcome to try one of our Colt automatics, Major."

"I'll stay with my Walther. A much sturdier weapon."

"When this is over we can have a side-by-side shoot-out," Schwarz commented, irritated at her patronizing attitude.

Pol decided it was time to stop the growing feud between Gadgets and the Russian woman. He turned to the general. "I knocked at your door earlier. You were out."

"I was over at the base supervising the unloading of some special equipment from our plane."

"You should have let us help unload it when we got in," Schwarz said, dropping the argument with Irina.

"Twenty thousand pounds?"

Ironman stared at the senior officer. "What the hell did you bring on the plane? A couple of nuclear bombs?"

"Exactly," Cassidy answered calmly. "Two Pershing 1-A missiles to be precise."

"*¡Dios!*" Pol exclaimed. "And we were sitting right on top of them?"

Irina looked bothered. "Who is guarding them?"

"They're not armed."

"But their guidance systems are very desirable," she reminded the senior officer. "A high price would be paid for them on the black market."

Defensively he answered, "We put them in a spare hangar until we can get them moved to China Lake later today. There's a team of MPs keeping an eye on them."

"The current price being offered for a missile of the Pershing class by groups not privileged to have access to them is a minimum of fifteen million dollars," Irina said.

"She's right, gentlemen," the general commented soberly. "There are a lot of people who'd like to get their hands on a Pershing, so I guess it's up to you to make sure they aren't stolen until we've had a chance to demonstrate to our new Russian friends how we plan to live up to our end of the treaty."

"Nobody will," Ironman said quietly. Everyone turned and stared at him. He wasn't smiling. Not on this side of hell.

20

Brigadier General Halloran showed up at the motel later that morning in full dress uniform with his silver star polished brightly. He was accompanied by his aide, Colonel Zearns, who carried a large leather briefcase. Both men were there to review plans for the next twenty-four hours.

The Russian major volunteered to make a fresh pot of coffee and disappeared into the small efficiency kitchen while the others pulled up chairs and gathered around the living room couch.

"Good flight, General?" Halloran asked Cassidy.

"I slept most of the way," Cassidy replied, then winked at his three traveling companions before continuing. "I had a pretty exhausting time before we took off."

"I suppose being in the Pentagon can wear you out, sir," Halloran commented, trying to mask his sarcasm.

Cassidy smiled patiently, then tapped the rows of ribbons on his chest. "I didn't win most of these fighting the political wars in Washington."

Halloran and his aide studied the citations, which included a Silver Star, a Purple Heart and combat ribbons from the Korean and Vietnam Wars.

"I thought you told me they wouldn't let you go up to the front lines," Gadgets commented, annoyed at himself for not having looked at Cassidy's medals closely.

The gray-haired man grinned like a little boy caught doing mischief. "As you know from last night, that never stopped me," he replied, and before Schwarz could make another remark, the general examined the ribbons on the jackets of the two military officers who had just arrived. "Looks like the two of you don't know how to stay out of fights, either."

Colonel Zearns grinned. "I never heard it put quite that way, sir."

"And probably you never will again, unless you get into a conversation with another nose tweaker like me," Cassidy commented, enjoying playing the role of the maverick. He turned to Halloran, who was sitting stiffly on one of the chairs. "What do we have to go over, General?"

Halloran turned to his aide and gestured for him to open the briefcase. Zearns understood immediately and fished out a manila folder stamped Confidential. He handed it to the general.

"Our latest intelligence," Halloran began, sounding rigidly formal as he studied the pages in the folder, "indicates that because of weather problems—not over the United States, I might add—the Russian team will arrive twelve hours later than originally planned."

"Get to the point," Cassidy snapped, annoyed at the long-winded introduction. "What does that mean?"

"It means," Halloran replied, becoming even more formal, "that they won't arrive until sometime tomorrow afternoon."

Irina came out of the kitchen carrying a tray of coffee. Gadgets jumped up and helped her set it down on the small dining table, then winked at her. She shook her head, then turned and looked at the brigadier general and his aide. "What provisions have you made for their safety when they arrive here?"

The sudden expression of hate and distrust on Halloran's face surprised Cassidy and the Able Team trio. In a surly tone he snapped, "A lot more than what your people will likely give us, *Major*!"

"Hey, we're supposed to be at peace, not war," Cassidy said in a conciliatory tone.

"That's what the orders from my commander-in-chief state," Halloran replied stiffly.

"Good. What about answering the major's question."

Colonel Zearns jumped in. "There will be tight security around the entire base until the Russian team departs Edwards. We've brought in extra men to protect both the Russian and the American teams."

"What about the American group?" Cassidy asked.

"They're arriving this afternoon as originally planned," Zearns replied.

"Contact them and reschedule their arrival to coincide with the Russians," Cassidy ordered.

"I don't see any need to change—" Halloran started to say.

"I don't care what you see or don't see, General Halloran. Just make sure they arrive when the Soviet team does," Cassidy snapped tersely.

Halloran stood up and snapped a salute at the senior officer from Washington. Cassidy looked up at him and shook his head. "Relax, man."

The brigadier general lowered his hand.

Cassidy turned to the colonel. "Would you make the call about the change in departure time, Colonel?" he asked.

Zearns jumped to his feet and looked around for a telephone.

"You can use the one in the kitchenette if you want privacy," Pol suggested softly.

The colonel vanished into the kitchenette.

"Now sit down, General," Cassidy ordered.

Hesitating for a moment, Halloran finally lowered his body back onto his chair.

"Tell us about your security arrangements."

"We'll have extra men at every gate. Not one of the seven thousand people who are stationed or work here gets on or off the base without permission, starting tonight. We have a specially selected ground crew who will handle flight arrivals and departures of the two teams."

Cassidy interrupted him. "I want everybody who has anything to do with handling the flights in and out to be checked by these three." He gestured at Pol, Gadgets and

Ironman. Turning to them, he added, "If that's okay with you."

Ironman answered for the three. "No sweat."

Halloran glanced at them and commented, "I'm certain we have qualified people—"

"That's an order!" Cassidy snapped.

The brigadier general stopped talking.

"Now what arrangements have you made to provide secured housing and demonstration sites for the visiting teams?"

"As you requested, we've arranged with the Naval Weapons Center at China Lake to provide a secured area for your demonstrations. We're bringing in Special Forces to help guard this motel."

"How does that sound to you?" Cassidy asked the three Able Team warriors.

"Okay, I guess," Pol replied.

"Except for the Special Forces types," Lyons said. "I don't think we need them."

"We can take care of ourselves, General," Gadgets reminded the senior officer.

Cassidy nodded and looked at Irina, who had not spoken. "Any comments, Major Tolstoy?"

"Captain Lyons and Major Schwarz have expressed my sentiments, General."

Halloran looked worried.

"You have a problem with that, General?" Cassidy asked him.

Zearns came back into the living room and answered quickly. "I think General Halloran just wants to make sure everything goes well, sir." He smiled. "May I make a suggestion?"

Cassidy nodded.

"Let us station a couple of jeeps with our security troops outside of the motel property where they won't make the visitors uncomfortable by being visible."

Cassidy turned to Ironman. "What do you think, Captain Lyons?"

Something didn't sound right to the blond warrior, but he couldn't put his finger on it. "I think," he finally replied, "that the general's men better be told to keep out of our way in case there's any trouble." He looked at Pol and Gadgets. "We have our own way of handling headaches."

Schwarz and Blancanales nodded in agreement.

Cassidy smiled and turned back to Halloran and his aide. "That's the way it's going to have to be, General. Understood?"

Halloran looked unhappy as he stood up and saluted Cassidy. "I'll make the necessary arrangements, General," he said coldly, then started to march out the front door, followed by Colonel Zearns.

"One more thing, General Halloran," Cassidy called out.

The brigadier general stopped and turned smartly back to the Irishman.

"When do you plan to move the missiles to China Lake?"

"In a little while, sir," he replied icily, then walked out of the motel apartment before Cassidy could ask any more questions.

"That is one angry man, General," Gadgets said.

"Perhaps he is kind to his mother," Irina said in a quiet voice filled with sarcasm.

Cassidy smiled at the exchange, then turned to Lyons. "You look bothered. Anything wrong?"

"I'm not sure," Ironman said. "Just a feeling in my guts that someone's eavesdropping on our plans."

"Have you checked the place out?" Cassidy asked, suddenly tense.

"No problem," Gadgets answered. "I screened the place from top to bottom. Nobody's planted anything or has got an external listening device focused on us," Gadgets answered.

"And if the science whiz says they haven't, you can count on it," Pol added.

"That's not what I was talking about," Ironman said. "It's just that I got the feeling Halloran wasn't on our wavelength. And that he's got somebody on the outside tuned in to his."

Gadgets looked at him, then walked into the kitchen.

"That sounds serious," Cassidy said. "Is there anything we should do about it?"

"It's being handled, General," Schwarz said, coming out of the kitchen. He turned to his two partners. "I called Bear. He'll have it checked out."

"Bear?" Cassidy asked.

"One of our staff people. If it's happening in the United States, he can find out about it. And fast," Pol explained.

"Before tomorrow, I hope," the general said.

"By this afternoon," Gadgets promised.

Cassidy stood up. "Then I suggest we get back together and talk about it when he gives you his report. I think I'll get over to the base and supervise moving the missiles to the test area." He started to leave, then remembered something. Turning to the three men, he asked, "Have you men got wheels?"

"No sweat," Ironman replied. "We called the base after you went to bed and they sent over a couple of jeeps. They're parked behind the motel."

"Good. See you later," the Irish officer said as he picked up his briefcase.

"I think I'll ride with you," Pol told him.

Cassidy looked surprised. "Got something to do at the base?"

"Absolutely. Keep an eye on your ass." Pol kneeled down near the metal boxes and selected the H&K-53 submachine gun, then searched through the box and found four 15-round magazines to fit it. Blancanales looked up at the general. "Interested in any of these?"

"Maybe my old favorite. That 12-gauge shotgun."

"Try this one instead," Pol said, handing him the six-round Mossberg slug gun. He found a box of shells for it and passed them up to the senior officer.

Cassidy smiled, then looked at the other three. "What are the rest of you planning to do?"

"I think I'll go back to my room and get a much-needed bath and nap. It's been a very tiring visit so far," Irina said as she stood up and stretched.

"How about you two?" Cassidy asked Lyons and Schwarz.

Gadgets started to speak. "Maybe the major and I ought to spend some time together, going over—"

"Forget it," Ironman said. "You and I are going to spend some time checking out the surrounding area and making sure there's no chance we'll have any unexpected guests."

He stood up and walked over to the metal boxes. Opening the first, he picked up a mini-Uzi and shoved three extra clips into his pant pocket. He also grabbed two speedloaders for his Python and tucked them into his other pocket. When he finally stood up, Ironman looked like his pants had the mumps.

Pol laughed as he stared at him. "Maybe you ought to get a shot for whatever's causing those lumps below your waist."

Uncharacteristically, Lyons came back with a straight-faced reply. "What's making me bulge, Homes, ain't the same thing that makes you bulge on occasion. What I've got won't kill me someday," he said pointedly, referring to Blancanales's constant passion for women.

"Neither will mine," the handsome man replied happily. "All it does is keep me young forever."

"Keep dreaming," Ironman cracked. Then he turned to Gadgets and asked, "Coming, Abbott?"

Schwarz nodded at the general and the Russian major, reached down into the opened box and picked up an M-16 and three magazines. "Right behind you, Costello," he said as he followed Ironman out the door.

21

Richie Lamantia watched as the men who had come with Hollings and his well-dressed companion zippered themselves into the combat uniforms he had acquired for them.

A long table had been set up so that he could display the various equipment they had ordered. As the customer and the Arab—the one Hollings had called Nidar—checked them over carefully, Richie kept his sales pitch going.

"Outside are two jeeps and a small Army van, all painted with camouflage designs and serial numbers indicating the vehicles are part of the motor depot at Fort Orr," he said.

Fort Orr was where two soldiers, desperate for money to cover their gambling debts, had stolen them. And the combat uniforms.

"And I personally checked," he bragged, "to make sure every piece of equipment is in working order. Yes, sir, gentlemen, you always get the best when you do business with Richie Lamantia."

Hollings seemed satisfied. He whispered something to Nidar, who turned to the other men and issued what appeared to be orders in some foreign language.

Expressionless, the men began to carry the weapons and other equipment out to the vehicles. Satisfied that the men were doing as requested, Hollings turn to Lamantia and, in a Southern accent, politely asked, "How much did y'all say it came to?"

The dealer handed him the calculator tape on which he had tallied the prices of the various items, inflated to reflect what he had guessed the customer would be willing to pay. Hollings glanced at it, then picked up an oversize suitcase and laid it on the long table. Opening it, he reached inside and took out five stacks of hundred-dollar bills. Richie stared at the rows of bills still in the suitcase. He estimated that there was almost a million dollars in hundred-dollar bills stacked neatly inside.

"Wasn't that the right amount?" Hollings asked, noticing the expression on Lamantia's face.

"Oh, sure, sure," Richie said, almost stuttering. Then he turned to two of his key men standing nearby and signaled for them to come over. He handed the money to them. "Count this out and let me know how much it comes to," he ordered.

The two men pulled folding bridge chairs up to the table, then sat down and started tallying the cash.

Nobody spoke until they were finished. One of them, the one Richie called Pete-O, looked over at Lamantia and nodded. "It's exactly the right amount," he called out.

Satisfied, Richie turned to Hollings and was surprised to see another stack of hundred-dollar bills in his hand. "We're even," he told him.

"Not quite," Hollings replied. "This should be enough to rent us space in your warehouse for two nights."

Richie showed his unhappiness at the request. "I dunno. We never rented—" Hollings handed him another stack of money. Richie stared at it, then looked at his customer. "We ain't got beds in here," he warned.

"I noticed some inflatable mattresses and surplus Army blankets stacked up in a corner," the customer said, adding more bills to the stack. "Our men can use those."

"Sure," Lamantia said, still stunned at the additional money he was receiving.

"And we'll need a private room for my use."

"There's nothing like that in here," Lamantia said, petulantly.

Nidar showed his annoyance. "We can find something more hospitable than this place."

Hollings didn't look perturbed. "Why don't you make sure the men are putting the right guns in the right vehicles?" he said, pointing to the sunlit parking area outside.

The Arab didn't move from where he was standing.

"This wasn't just a suggestion," Hollings barked.

Nidar was about to reply, then changed his mind and walked outside to the parking area. After he had gone, Hollings glanced at the locked weapons storeroom. "How about in there?"

"That's off-limits."

"Worried I might steal whatever you keep in there?"

"Ain't that," the gun dealer muttered. "I keep a rottweiler in there. What do I do with him?"

"Y'all can just chain him to the wall during the time I'm in there," the ex-KGB agent said.

Lamantia was about to say no when Hollings waved a small stack of money in his face. "This will buy him a lot of horse meat to make up for any hurt feelings he has, and leave a few extra daddy greenbacks for y'all to spend on yourselves," Hollings commented.

The hundred-dollar bills were hypnotic. Lamantia couldn't turn his eyes away from them. Finally he lowered his head and mumbled, "You got yourself a deal," as he grabbed the money.

"Good. Don't forget to put a mattress and blankets in there, too," the customer commented, then asked, "Y'all got a private phone I can use?"

He saw the hesitant expression on the gun dealer's face.

"It's a local call to an old buddy who's up at Edwards Air Force Base."

Lamantia shrugged and waved a hand magnanimously toward the room in which he did his bookkeeping. "Use the one in my office. No charge."

Nidar chose that moment to walk back into the warehouse. "We're ready to move out when you are, old boy," he called out in an English accent.

"Why don't you get into your uniform? I'll be with you in a few minutes," Hollings called back as he walked into the office.

Through the meshed fencing the former intelligence officer could be seen dialing a phone, then talking into it. For a moment he seemed to be having a heated discussion with someone on the other end of the line. Then he mumbled something and hung up. He changed into an officer's uniform and walked toward the Arab. "Now I'm ready," he announced.

"Everything okay, old boy?"

"Damn straight it is," Hollings beamed. "We hit an extra jackpot."

He saw the look of curiosity on Nidar's face.

"Turns out our people brought a couple of Pershing nuclear missiles with them—for demonstration purposes." He beamed at the Arab. "Know anybody who might want to buy them?" he asked.

Before Nidar could reply, Lamantia jumped in. "I got a customer who'd pay up to—" He hesitated before continuing while he tried to remember how much the skinhead had offered him. "I bet he'd pay as much as two million bucks for one."

Hollings looked at Nidar's suddenly angry expression and stopped him before he could say anything. "Sounds like a reasonable offer to me. I'll let you know after we get our hands on them."

Lamantia looked pleased. This business deal was getting sweeter all the time. "Anything I can do for you guys, just holler," he offered, trying to pretend that his bid on the missiles was nothing more than a way of being hospitable.

"We'll do that," Hollings promised, smiling happily. "You're a helluva lot nicer than your reputation." He turned to the Arab. "Guess it's just about time we got the show on the road. We've got a man to meet for a cup of coffee. And there's a lady I'll bet is just dying to see us," he said, still in a good mood. "Or is it the other way round?"

He looked back at the gun dealer. "See you later," he said, then turned and led the other man out of the warehouse.

"GOOD TO SEE YOU AGAIN, SIR," Hollings said in his best Southern accent, standing and saluting as General Halloran and his aide walked into the empty coffee shop located in the Antelope Valley south of Rosamond and just off Highway 14. The ex-Russian intelligence agent had put on a pair of metal-rimmed eyeglasses with clear glass lenses as part of his disguise.

The brigadier general looked around to make sure they were alone before he and Colonel Zearns slid into the booth to join Hollings. He stared at the man he had met only once before. Hollings looked different. Perhaps it was the major's combat uniform he was wearing. Or the fact that he had changed his hair color. No, there was something else about him that was new.

He didn't look as intense as he had the first time they had met a week ago. If he hadn't examined him closely, he wouldn't have recognized him. He hoped that was also true of the MPs around the base.

"I saw the men you brought with you waiting outside," the general said quietly after a waitress served coffee to the three of them in their booth and walked back behind the counter.

"Look military enough for you?" Hollings asked.

"They look like a bunch of Arabs to me," the senior officer said, his face revealing his feelings about Middle Easterners.

"They are. But they all live here now."

Halloran made a face.

"They won't be here for long," the ex-KGB agent said warmly.

"Where are they going afterward?" the colonel asked.

"Back to where they came from," Hollings said, sounding certain of his promise. Back to whatever God created those animals, he added to himself silently.

Halloran grimaced, then turned to Zearns. "Give him those items he wanted."

The colonel reached into his briefcase and passed a large, bulging manila envelope across the table. "Your ID tags. We went through our personnel files to find pictures of men who looked like they could have come from that part of the world."

Hollings opened the envelope and glanced inside.

"There's two tags for commissioned officers. You said you wanted IDs for a first lieutenant and a major."

"Perfect," Hollings acknowledged as he examined several of them. "These should get us into any place on the base."

"Absolutely. The MPs have been alerted that there is a Special Forces group coming in to help with security," Zearns reported.

"What's the latest scheduling?" Hollings asked.

Halloran nodded to his aide to review the revised plans. The colonel took out a handwritten list and started reading from it. "We haven't had time to get this typed up yet," he apologized as he talked about the new ETAs for the Russian and American teams. And the plans to demonstrate the dismantling at China Lake.

"Will these IDs get us in there?" Hollings asked.

"No problem. They've been alerted," the colonel said.

"Where are you housing the teams?"

Zearns looked at his superior, who nodded his permission to continue. Turning back to the man in the major's uniform, he said, "We've taken over a motel ten miles north of here and just off Highway 14. It's called the Mojave View. The only civilians there are the manager, three housekeepers who change the sheets and clean up the rooms and an old Indian, who's a combination gardener and handyman. They've closed down the restaurant, so we'll be sending in food from the base commissary three times a day."

"Why aren't they eating at the base?" Hollings asked.

"Orders from the Pentagon were to keep them totally isolated from anybody who isn't involved in this mission."

"You don't happen to have a layout of the motel with you?"

Zearns nodded. "I brought one along in case you asked." He reached into his bag and took out a reduced version of the architect's plans for the two-story motel. He handed it to the man across the table.

"Who's staying where?" Hollings asked.

Zearns referred to some handwritten notes, then took out a pen and pointed out the apartment where the three "bodyguards" were being housed. And the two-room suite Cassidy was using.

"What about the Russian woman? Which is her room?"

Zearns pointed to a large corner room on the ground level. "She occupies this one in the northeast corner of the motel."

Hollings turned the plans around so that he could study them. He seemed to be memorizing the locations of various sections of the building. Finally he pointed at the curved driveway that led from the country road onto the motel property. "Is this the only way in and out of the motel?"

"Yes," Zearns said.

"What's around the motel?"

"The Mojave Desert. There's nothing closer than three or four miles. Except for the garbage that tourists keep dumping around the area."

"Where is everybody right now?"

"I don't know. Except for General Cassidy and one of the bodyguards who showed up at the base, just as we were leaving," the colonel said.

"Any reason to believe the rest of them have left the motel?"

"No. They brought several metal cases with them, which were spread around the living room when we met with them this morning. They looked like they planned to spend time checking out whatever was inside of them."

Hollings stood and picked up the check the waitress had left before she disappeared into the room behind the counter. As they walked out of the coffee shop, Hollings glanced at the two jeeps and the military van that were parked on the blind side of the eating place, partially hidden from the state highway, then turned to Halloran. "Oh, by the way, where are you storing the missiles they brought with them?" he asked casually.

"In a hangar on the base," Halloran replied as they continued walking toward the vehicles. "Under heavy guard. You're not planning to...steal them? That wasn't part of our agreement."

Hollings looked at the men in the jeep, then turned back to the two officers and said, "Remember the old expression 'situations alter cases, just like noses alter faces'?"

Zearns backed away from the man. "Now hold on a minute. Keeping the Commies out of America is one thing, but stealing missiles is something else. You try to pull that off and I'll blow the whistle, even if it means my being in the guardhouse for the rest of my life," he warned. "I mean it, mister!"

"I know you do," Hollings sighed.

The former KGB agent gestured to Nidar, who looked up and down the highway to make sure they weren't being watched, then revealed the Uzi with an Invicta sound suppressor screwed to its muzzle that he'd been keeping out of sight. Calmly the Arab squeezed off four 9 mm rounds and listened to the soft whoosh of the copper clads as they leaped from the muzzle of the automatic into the stomachs of the two officers.

Hollings pulled out a 9 mm Glock silenced automatic from the buttoned leather holster he wore on the military belt hanging around his waist and aimed carefully at the older officer's temple. He pulled the trigger twice and listened to the muffled explosion rip a hole in the man's head, then pointed the automatic at the still form of the colonel and fired again.

He studied the gaping, bleeding wounds in both bodies. "Better safe than sorry," he told Nidar quietly, sliding the handgun back into his holster. "Have one of your men drive their jeep and let's get their bodies into the van."

After the Arab's people had loaded the dead men into the rear of the van and covered them with blankets, Hollings climbed into the rear of the jeep and sat next to Nidar. "Now let's keep our next appointment," he said. "Then we can all go home."

As they drove out of the coffee shop lot, Hollings had a smile of anticipation on his face. This was one appointment he had waited a long time to keep.

22

Lyons and Gadgets struggled through the sand that had blown across the dirt country road that paralleled California Highway 14. This was their third swing around the area, and so far they had seen no sign of life. Neither friend nor foe.

"I wonder when the hell those Special Forces types are supposed to show up?" Gadgets asked, twisting the steering wheel to keep the four-wheel-drive vehicle from skidding into the mounds of soft sand that bordered the road. He had his M-16 propped next to him, ready to grab and use instantly.

"Do we really need them?" Ironman asked.

"No," Schwarz admitted. "But I'd like to know they're earning their monthly pay." He stopped the jeep and pulled himself up on his seat to get a better view. "Tell you one thing," he said as he stared at the heat that radiated from the desert. "Being out here can sure get you thirsty."

"We'll pick up a couple of six-packs later," Lyons promised.

"Better make that more than a couple. That Cassidy is Irish," Gadgets suggested, grinning.

"Let's take one more swing around. There are a couple of dirt roads we haven't checked out yet," Ironman said, gripping his mini-Uzi tightly to keep it from bouncing out of the jeep.

"Work, work, work. Is that all you think about?" Schwarz complained. "Who's back at the motel protecting our Russian guest?"

Lyons grinned. "She looks like she can take care of herself without your assistance."

"But I'll bet she prefers having help."

The Ironman shook his head in mock despair. "What are we going to do with you now that you've discovered girls?"

Schwarz made a face. "Just shut up and let's get on with our work," he muttered as he put the vehicle in gear and raced down the road deeper into the desert.

IRINA MALKOVA TOLSTOY had just finished taking a long, hot shower when she heard the sound of vehicles outside. She wrapped the huge bath sheet around her waist and stood in front of the steam-clouded bathroom mirror.

The military bodyguards, she thought as she dried her hair with the small dryer she'd purchased at the airport in New York. She decided she'd better get dressed.

She studied the uniform she had hung in the bathroom in hopes of steaming the wrinkles out. Perhaps she could put on some jeans and a T-shirt for now. No, she decided. It would never do to be seen by the American military people out of uniform.

The three men from Able Team had seen her in casual clothes—Gadgets in less than that. Of course, she reminded herself, they weren't really soldiers. At least not the kind of soldiers who wore uniforms as part of their job.

What a crazy world this was, she told herself as she fastened the small holster to her thigh, tucked the small Beretta Jetfire into it, pulled on her skirt, then took her shirt from its hanger and put it on.

She had been taught to hate groups like Able Team. And here she was admiring what they were trying to do all by themselves.

They were killers. But every day they put their own lives at risk, willingly, for a cause in which they believed.

Like herself.

She pulled on her uniform jacket and buttoned it, then checked herself in the mirror. The hair. It was hanging loose. She reached for the barrette and pulled the long red strands back behind her head when she heard the knock at her door.

She hesitated and then reached for her Walther automatic before moving toward the door. "Who is it?" she asked loudly.

"Major Houseman. I'm in command of the security forces assigned to your group," the male voice answered in a soft Southern accent.

She put the gun back in her handbag and went to the door. The man standing in the open area outside was in a combat uniform—camouflage fatigues, boots and helmet. On his shoulders he wore the insignia of an American major. "May I come in?" he asked.

There was something uncomfortably familiar about him. She stared at the spectacles that covered his eyes.

And recognized him.

Before she could turn to retrieve the automatic, the man pointed a compact Glock automatic at her. "Major Tolstoy?"

"I recognize you, Lubankov," she said, standing still. Her voice reflected the disgust she still felt for him.

"Of course you do, Doctor. How are things back at Dzerzhinsky Square? Shall we go?"

She choked back the nausea. "I'm not going with you."

Hollings whipped the gun across her face. The Russian woman fell to the floor, forcing herself not to scream from the pain, then moaned as he kicked her in her side before he yanked her back onto her feet. "Yes, you are," he said coldly.

"So you can kill me?"

"Perhaps later. But that's not what I had in mind for now," he said as he resumed smiling.

He forced her to precede him out onto the walkway that rimmed the motel, prodding her in the back with the automatic each time she hesitated.

Three jeeps and a small military van were waiting at the side of the motel. She stared at the uniformed men sitting in them, recognizing their features as Middle Eastern.

"So you now work for the Arabs," she said bitterly, walking as slowly toward them as Hollings would permit.

"No. They work for me."

They reached one of the jeeps. A handsome man wearing first lieutenant's bars on his shoulders sat on one of the back seats.

Hollings turned to the man. "They're expecting a group of Special Forces at the base to drive the truck with the missile and guard it. Send four of your men. You stay here with four and wait for the bodyguard and the general to return. When you're done with them—including the two bodyguards who must be somewhere in the motel—meet us back at Lamantia's place. I'll take the rest of the men, the bodies and the girl there with me now."

Nidar nodded, then ordered four of his men to go with Hollings.

The former KGB officer shoved Irina into the van, then climbed in next to her and studied her face. She turned her eyes away and stared over her shoulder at the two bodies covered by Army blankets.

"They weren't useful any longer, so I got rid of them," he commented casually.

Irina shuddered.

BY THE TIME Ironman and Gadgets got back to the motel, there were two jeeps filled with Special Forces troops wearing combat uniforms parked on the side of the road near the building.

Schwarz waved at them as he drove past and was surprised that none of them waved back.

"The Special Forces have sure lowered their standards since my time," he commented to Lyons.

"Don't sweat it. Everybody else has, too," Ironman replied. "When was the last time you got a letter delivered the next day, even locally?"

Gadgets nodded as he parked the car in front of their door.

Ironman jumped out and started for their apartment.

"Hold it. Let me see if the major would like to join us," Schwarz said.

He walked to her room and knocked on the door. There was no answer. He called out her name. No reply.

Looking disappointed, he turned around and walked back to Ironman, who had opened their door. "Either she's sound asleep or she's gone for a stroll."

"The Special Forces men may know," Lyons suggested.

Gadgets turned his head and looked down the driveway. One of the jeeps was visible. He waved to the first lieutenant who stood at the side of the vehicle talking to the three men inside it. Finally he got his attention. "Did you see a Russian major? A woman with red hair?" he shouted.

The officer shook his head, then turned around to continue his conversation.

Lyons saw a hint of a lost look on the electronics whiz's face. "Let's get inside and see if there's a message on your portable gizmo from Bear."

Gadgets had forgotten that he'd asked Bear to check into Halloran's connections. If there was any information, Bear would have left a signal for them to call back on the portable secure cellular telephone that Schwarz had helped develop for Able Team.

As suspected, the tiny red light was flashing on the plastic attaché case that held the cellular phone unit. Gadgets used the standard routine for telephone contact from the field. He contacted the first of a series of blind telephone numbers and spoke the code for the day each time he heard the beep of a recording machine. Finally he heard Kurtzman's voice.

"Hold it until I switch to the speaker phone so Ironman can also hear," Schwarz said, and set the switches on the unit. "Go ahead, Bear. Now we can both hear you."

"Where's Pol?"

"Acting as a bodyguard to General Cassidy, who turned out to be one hell of a fine man to have in a fight."

"Like you reported last night."

"Exactly. So what did you learn?" Gadgets asked.

"Halloran has been associated with a lot of right-wing crazies, including our friends in the ARC."

The Aryan Right Coalition was a skinhead movement with leanings toward violence and torture reminiscent of the hellish years when the Nazis ran Germany and much of Europe. Able Team had done battle with elements of the movement several times, destroying key members but never eliminating the real powers behind the paramilitary organization.

"He went off the deep end when some left-wing terrorists hit our embassy in Beirut several years ago and chewed up his only daughter with their bullets during their attack. Ever since then he's been speaking openly against trusting the Russians. It cost him a couple of promotions despite his military record."

"This man Lubankov who calls himself Hollings is a Russian," Gadgets protested. "Why would Halloran get mixed up with a dirtbag like him?"

"He doesn't know he's Russian. Lubankov puts on a Southern accent that would make you believe he was raised on one of those fancy plantations in Mississippi or Georgia. But hold off with your comments. There's a lot more."

Schwarz glanced at Ironman, who looked disturbed by what he had already heard. "We're all ears."

"And no mouth, please, for the next few minutes," Kurtzman requested. "Hollings is being backed on this particular action by an international banker in Washington. A guy named Peter Mallincott. According to the DEA files, they suspect he's laundering money for the Medellín, Cali and Jalisco Syndicates."

Gadgets whistled. "This is getting crazy. Why the hell is this Mallincott involved?"

"That's the cute part. His bank has made loans around the world to defense contractors. Several billions according to the CIA and State Department files. If the disarmament treaty becomes operational, he stands to lose the money."

"What about Hollings?" Ironman asked.

"He was spotted at Dulles International Airport this morning in the company of another man getting on an American flight for L.A.," Kurtzman said. "The man he was with is a diplomat from one of the small Arab nations. His name's Ibrahim Nadir and he's better known as a terrorist leader who rents his followers out to the highest bidder."

"How many men did he have with him?" Schwarz asked, drumming his fingers on the table in frustration.

"None," Bear reported. "But they could have gone out on different flights."

"Any clues as to where these sweet people are hiding?" Lyons asked.

"Hollings has done business before with an arms dealer named Richie Lamantia, who operates out of a small desert town near your location." He gave him the address.

"Anything else to tell us?" Gadgets asked.

"I can send you a photograph of Nidar if you set the fax machine on your little gizmo," he offered.

Schwarz turned on the unit and attached a wire from the cellular phone. In a few minutes the photograph Bear was sending from the Shenandoah Valley in Virginia would be transmitted and printed. "Ready," Gadgets announced. "Signing off for now."

He set the phone back on its base and watched as the fax machine made the connection with their portable phone. The end of the roll of treated paper under the unit's cover began to appear. When the photograph had been reproduced, Gadgets tore off the page and studied the face on the paper. "Recognize the guy?" he asked Lyons.

Ironman shook his head. "Looks like a slicker with that fancy mustache," he commented.

Gadgets knew he had seen the face before. But where? He kept staring at the picture until he remembered. "I know this guy," he said in a shocked voice.

"Who is he?"

"He's the first lieutentant who's supposed to be protecting us!"

"You sure?"

"I'll stake my life on it."

Lyons leaned down and opened one of the large metal cases. Inside was the assortment of assault weapons and boxes of cartridges. He looked them over and substituted the Galil assault rifle for the mini-Uzi he'd been carrying. He snapped in a magazine loaded with copper-jacketed 5.56 high-velocity rounds and then shoved three additional magazines into a pant pocket.

"Let's stake his life on it instead. Grab your weapons and let's go get the bastard!" Lyons said grimly as he stood up.

"What about the major?" Gadgets asked, showing his concern.

"She's safer where she is than with us," Lyons said. "Ready?"

Gadgets bent down and grabbed a 40 mm fragmentation and an incendiary grenade. Clipping them to his belt, he picked up the AR-15A2 Delta H-Bar countersniper and checked to make sure it had a full magazine. He decided to carry it instead of the M-16 he had taken with him on their inspection rounds because of its lighter weight and shorter length.

He quickly searched through the other metal case and found what he was looking for—three magazines filled with rounds for his 10 mm Delta Elite. He was grateful that Cowboy hadn't forgotten.

There was a fat, dark metal cylinder lying near them. Schwarz noticed the handwritten note taped to it: "For your new toy just in case you need it. Cowboy."

Gadgets recognized it—a sound suppressor for his 10 mm Delta Elite. He wondered why Kissinger had wasted space sending it along. But he had learned not to question the armorer's weapons instincts, so he slipped the thick silencer into his already crowded pocket along with the magazines.

"Now I'm ready," he announced as he stood up. "Let's go have a talk with the scum."

23

The jeep was nowhere in sight when they rushed out of their apartment. Surprised, Ironman and Gadgets ran down the driveway to see if it had pulled back. But the road was empty.

"Where the hell did they go?" Gadgets asked.

He didn't have to wait long for the answer. Behind them the still desert air was ruptured by the sudden roar of an engine. They turned and saw the jeep rushing down the motel driveway at them from where it had been hiding at the side of the building.

Two of the three uniformed men in it started spraying 9 mm slugs from the AK-47s they pressed against their shoulders. Their Middle Eastern features were twisted into expressions of hate as they watched a round tear into Gadgets's left side and spin him around.

Lyons dived to the ground to get out of the way of the military vehicle, grabbing Schwarz to pull him down also. Gadgets jerked his arm free and stood his ground, daring them to hit him.

He waited until the jeep was almost on top of him before he washed the front of the vehicle with round after round of armor-piercing slugs from his AR-15 counter-sniper rifle.

He could feel the hot metal barrel burning deep grooves into his palms as 5.56 slugs rushed at the jeep from the muzzle of his powerful weapon at a speed of twelve hundred feet per second.

The front windshield shattered into fragments, driving shards of glass into the driver's face and eyes. The jeep kept rushing at him, out of control, and Gadgets finally had to dive into the sand at the side of the road to avoid being crushed.

Ironman had dropped the Galil and hauled out his .357 Python. Without bothering to steady it with both hands, he started pumping hollowpoints at the two men in the rear before they could turn and fire back.

The lower jaw of one of the men dissolved as the slugs exploded into fragments inside of his mouth. He doubled over and fell to the floor of the jeep's rear seat. The second man turned and glared at Lyons as he locked his finger on the trigger of his assault rifle.

Ironman's first shot at him tore into his larynx. The would-be assassin dropped his weapon as he sped on his journey to whatever heaven Nadir had promised him. The jeep ran across the road and onto the desert, bucking like a blinded burro until it finally spun around in the soft sand and came to a stop.

"Are you okay, Homes?" Lyons asked as he ran over to where Gadgets was lying.

A red stain began to seep through the side and rear of Schwarz's military pants. "Fine. Except I think I'm going to be sitting on a rubber doughnut for a while. How about you?"

Lyons touched the bleeding scratches on the side of his face. "I just need a little plastic surgery." He looked at the pain on Gadgets's face. "Maybe I should get the base to send an ambulance."

Gadgets held out his hand. Lyons grabbed it and helped his partner to his feet. Schwarz staggered unsteadily for a moment, then caught himself. "Maybe after we're finished," he replied, trying to keep his voice from revealing how much he was hurting. He looked at the Galil lying on the ground and the Python in Ironman's hand. "I guess you can't teach an old dog new tricks." He turned his head and looked across the sand at the stalled jeep. "How many did we get?"

"Three, I think."

Lyons walked across the road and onto the sand, tightly gripping his .357 revolver, ready to use it in case it was needed. He glanced inside the military vehicle and checked the bodies. The three men were dead. Every instinct in his body told him he was looking at empty, broken bags of skin and bones that once contained the angry lives of dedicated killers. He turned and walked back to Gadgets. "They won't try to kill anybody anymore."

Schwarz looked satisfied. "I'll call Bear and have him arrange for a garbage removal service before we go and find the rest of them."

Lyons nodded. "I wonder why Irina didn't come out when she heard the shooting?" he asked as he retrieved the assault rifle and threw it over his shoulder along with the mini-Uzi.

"Let's stop on the way to our apartment and ask her," Gadgets suggested.

He started to lead the way up the driveway to the motel and almost fell when the pain in his side threw him off balance. Lyons moved quickly to his side and put an arm around his waist.

Moving slowly, they climbed the slight incline and headed for Major Tolstoy's door. It was open. Gadgets looked at Ironman. "I could have sworn it was closed when I stopped by before."

"Unless she opened it since then," Lyons said.

Gadgets stopped at the doorway and called out, "Irina?" There was no answer. He tried again. "Major Tolstoy?"

The two men exchanged glances. Both knew something was wrong.

Gadgets loaded a fresh magazine into his AR-15 while Lyons replaced the empty shells in his Python, using a speedloader. Schwarz cocked his assault rifle and kicked open the door. A sheet of 9 mm firepower sprayed the opening from the inside. Gadgets and Ironman jumped to the sides, getting out of the way of the angry slugs just in time.

"That isn't the major," Gadgets said. "She wouldn't have missed."

"Want to try a forward rush?" Ironman asked.

"After I do this," Schwarz said.

He pulled a 40 mm incendiary grenade from his belt and yanked the pin, counted to ten and tossed it into the room. The unbearable heat and glare from the burning phosphorus increased the temperature inside the room by at least thirty degrees. They could hear the screeches of whoever was inside.

"Now!" Gadgets yelled.

The two men rushed into the smoldering room and braved the eye-searing fumes to search through the thick smoke and flames for whatever invaders were inside.

Gagging from the smoke and phosphorous stench, Gadgets looked in the closets and under the scorched bed. He saw the contents of Irina's bag strewn across the torched bedspread. Her gun, the 9 mm Walther, was also there.

She wouldn't have left without it, not unless somebody had forced her to leave.

"She isn't here," a coughing voice gasped. "By now she should be dead, like you two bastards!"

The two wary fighters spun around and saw the outline of a man leaning heavily against the burning bathroom door, pointing a full-size Uzi at them. His fury-filled eyes glowed eerily against his blackened skin as he forced his heat-sealed hand open and worked a finger against the trigger.

"For God!" he shrieked, pulling the trigger.

Before the 9 mm slugs could hit them, both Able Team commandos jumped aside and then, in tandem, unleashed their awesome firepower into the terrorist's body until he dropped the weapon and sank to the floor.

Blinking constantly to wash the chemicals from the grenade out of his eyes, Ironman cautiously checked to make sure the man was dead. What had been his chest was now a huge, open cavern, revealing fractured bones and torn bits of flesh.

Gadgets joined Lyons and stared at what was left of the face. The faint outline of a thin mustache was still visible. He recognized him as the man in the photograph Bear had faxed from Stony Man Farm—Ibrahim Nidar.

"They've taken her with them," Gadgets reported as they left the smoldering room, coughing and choking from the acrid fumes and flames, and headed back to their own apartment.

Lyons nodded but said nothing. He kept remembering the FBI female agent he had loved whom Gadgets couldn't save from being killed.

After Gadgets finished using the secured cellular phone unit to give Stony Man Farm the report, he hung up and commented to Ironman, "I wish Bear had known how many of them there were so we would know when it's over."

"It's over when they stop shooting at us," Lyons said, still wheezing from the chemicals he had inhaled.

"Yeah, but if you think of it that way, it won't be over till we're dead," he commented as he moved toward the bathroom.

They tried to rinse the phosphorous from their eyes and skin as best they could, then Gadgets reluctantly submitted to Ironman's insistence that he let him cleanse and bandage the wounds.

Ironman made Schwarz pull down his pants and lie facedown on the couch while he retrieved the first-aid kit Cowboy had packed for them. Washing the dirt and congealing blood away from where the slugs had grazed Gadgets, he carefully covered the wound with a combination painkiller and antibiotic cream that Brognola had friends of his at Walter Reed Army Hospital specially blend for them.

"Doesn't look like anything major except that you'll be sitting on your cheek for a while," he commented as he taped a thick gauze pad over the angry-looking wound.

"Thanks," Gadgets said as he pulled his pants up. He started for the door, then changed his mind and went back to the metal cases. He replaced the incendiary grenade, then saw two of the new carbon steel knives in Velcro sheaths and a pair of Invicta sound suppressors.

Bending stiffly, Schwarz strapped one of the blades to his leg, then picked up a sound suppressor and screwed it to the end of his specially threaded AR-15. He glanced at his Able Team colleague and saw that he was doing the same.

They left the apartment after changing into the gum sole shoes they had packed and headed for the address Bear had given them earlier. They were sure that the Russian major had been taken to the arms dealer's warehouse.

Schwarz had insisted on driving. "We should let Pol know what's up," he said as he raced the jeep down State Highway 14.

Ironman nodded. He took out the small communicator Schwarz had helped develop and tried to signal Blancanales.

There was no response. Lyons was a little concerned. Pol had the general with him. He'd try again in a few minutes.

As the Able Team warriors approached the cutoff road that led to Lamantia's place, Ironman thought of something. "How come you were so sure the major wasn't in there?" he asked.

"That's easy. Hollings was still alive," Schwarz replied, pushing the jeep to its maximum speed and taking the turn on the two tires on the right side.

Lyons decided no comment was necessary.

24

Blancanales was racing to catch up with the speeding truck hauling the two missiles when he heard the communicator in his pocket buzz. There was no time to answer it right now. He let it buzz until it finally stopped.

Four killers were trying to get away with the pair of Pershing missiles the general and he had been escorting to China Lake.

He glanced quickly at the gray-haired general sitting next to him. If the expression on Cassidy's face was any indication, the four men didn't stand a chance.

Everything had seemed normal when they had arrived at the base an hour ago. As expected, two of the Special Forces men Halloran had brought in were sitting behind the wheel of the long truck, ready to leave. Another pair were sitting in a jeep, carrying M-16s.

It was only after they had driven out through the major gates and onto the access road that the trouble had begun. When the truck reached State Highway 14, it was supposed to turn right and drive north toward China Lake. Instead the driver made a left and headed south.

Pol and the general had been riding rear guard.

"We'd better warn him that he's going the wrong way," Cassidy said.

Pol rammed down on the accelerator and raced alongside the truck so that he could reach the cab. "You're going the wrong way," he shouted up to the driver.

The dark-faced man behind the wheel opened the window, stared at him, then closed it again and continued driving.

"Something's wrong," Cassidy said.

"Very wrong," Pol agreed. "I think we've been suckered."

Cassidy grabbed the 12-gauge Mossberg slug gun and raised the twenty-four-inch-long weapon to his shoulder. Before he could fire Pol whipped out his .45 ACP Colt automatic with his right hand and fired a one-handed warning shot at the driver's window.

The slug chopped out a chunk of safety glass, and the driver responded by accelerating.

"How the hell are we going to stop him with this jeep?" the general asked.

"David and Goliath style," Pol said. "Start pumping rounds at the driver's window."

Cassidy pressed the 12-gauge against his shoulder and started squeezing off rounds of the hourglass-shaped cartridges at the front windshield. The first round created a spiderweb of fractured glass as it ricocheted off the metal frame around the windshield. The next two rounds exploded through the window and door of the truck cab. The driver squealed with pain as the slug tore a huge chunk of flesh out of his shoulder.

"Buffalo Bill couldn't have done better!" Blancanales shouted. "Hit him again!"

The truck began to swerve out of control as Cassidy fired another round. The wildly fired slug ricocheted inside the cab and dug into the driver's neck.

The terrorist slumped over the wheel, then slid down out of sight just as Blancanales's communicator started buzzing again. Pol quickly exchanged locations and reports with Ironman, then concentrated on trying to avoid being crushed by the runaway truck.

The jeep with the other two uniformed men cut around the rear of the truck. The killer in the passenger seat started firing an M-16 at them.

"Here, quick, let's change places," Pol shouted, lifting himself up so that the general could slide under him.

When he felt the general's foot on the accelerator, he lifted his, then released the steering wheel and slid over to let the senior officer handle the driving. Rolling into the passenger seat, Blancanales reached down and grabbed his H&K-53. Twisting around, he rammed the compact attack weapon against his shoulder and started showering the windshield of the other jeep with hot lead.

The windshield crumbled into slivers under the hammering of 9 mm armor-piercing rounds. Utilizing an instinct born of experience, Pol guessed at the windage and fired at the passenger with the Heckler & Koch. The man's features vanished under a mask of blood.

"Bank shot!" Blancanales shouted, using his H&K-53 as a pool stick as he prepared to fire again.

The jeep's driver shrieked at the burning pain and died an instant later. The vehicle swerved across the road and turned over as it raced into the soft sand on the side of the road.

"Let's get these babies up to China Lake," Cassidy said, jumping out of the jeep and running for the stalled truck.

"Wait!" Pol shouted.

He was too late. The second man came around the side of the huge vehicle and started blasting slugs at them. Cassidy twisted and flew across the road as two rounds burned into his shoulder. Pol sprayed the assassin with a shower of burning metal, slicing him in half, then ran to where the general had fallen.

The older man opened his eyes and smiled weakly. "I think I should have stuck to paper shuffling," he gasped, then closed his eyes against the pain.

At least he was still alive, Blancanales thought gratefully as he lowered Cassidy's head and got up.

The general needed an ambulance. And fast.

He remembered the short wave in their jeep that connected to the base. He ran to it and contacted the base dispatcher.

Explaining the situation, he listened as the dispatcher ordered an ambulance for the general and troops to get the truck to China Lake.

He returned to Cassidy's side and made a pillow out of his jacket. Gently he shoved it under the older man's head. "Hang on. They're on the way," he said.

"Damn. And I was going to ask you if you'd like a new recruit for your team," Cassidy said, trying to force a smile onto his face.

"We can check out the rest of your credentials later," Pol said. He heard the sounds of sirens coming closer. "Okay if I desert and see if I can give the other guys a hand?"

"Sure. And apologize that I'm not there to help save their asses," Cassidy said before he closed his eyes again.

HOLLINGS SNEERED at the naked woman lying semiconscious on the inflated rubber mattress. He felt safer now that her hands were tied together with a length of thick hawser rope.

He stared triumphantly at the long red hair he had hacked into uneven shorter lengths with the seven-inch blade of his bayonet. Her face and jaw were covered with dark bruises and clotted blood from where the former KGB assassin had pummeled her into submission.

Step by step he had expertly stripped away every aspect of her pride. She had struggled when he'd begun to tear away the gray-blue skirt, desperately trying to stop him. But he had torn her hands away and ripped the skirt and half-slip from her firm, warm body.

As a precaution he had checked her teeth, forcing a piece of dowelling between her lips. He didn't want a cyanide capsule that was buried in a filling to spoil his plans.

It had taken him a long time to achieve this victory. Now he was going to turn her into a empty shell before he killed her. He wasn't finished yet. There was still her mind. Before he was done he wanted her to beg him to take her life.

The animal behind him began to growl in a deep-throated, angry tone. Hollings turned and studied the enraged rottweiler that strained furiously to get loose from the thick tempered steel chain Lamantia had used to prevent it from breaking free.

The ex-KGB agent looked around at the cases of weapons and ammunition that lined the walls of the inner room Lamantia used as a storeroom. He himself couldn't have found a better place for the death chamber of the woman who was so expert at killing.

He glanced at the sliding doors to the room. He had left them half-open deliberately to make her humiliation more complete, knowing that a dozen men were listening to her every moan and whimper.

The two bodyguards who had been assigned to protect her didn't concern him. By now the Arab and his men had killed them and should be on their way back to the warehouse.

There were, in fact, only a few things left to be done—after he was finished with her. Plant the documents on her body, put the bodies of the two officers near her and then fly back to Mexico.

He turned back and stared at the woman again. Her eyes were still filled with hate. She needed another lesson in submission.

He kneeled and grabbed a handful of the butchered red hair. Yanking her face close to his, he waited for her cries of pain. She bit her lip until blood flowed, but made no sound.

Dropping her, he slapped her face. "Bitch! You'll cry before I'm done!" he shouted angrily.

She looked up at his face and spat a mixture of phlegm and blood at him. He closed his hand into a fist and hit her left cheekbone, feeling her skin buckle under the impact. Involuntarily she cried out.

"You'll do a lot more crying before I'm done," he promised, losing his Southern accent. "And begging," he added with a vicious smile.

The woman's head fell back onto the mattress. She closed her eyes against the pain and turned her face away from him. He could see the tears running down her cheeks. This was how he wanted her.

25

Ironman and Gadgets had parked their jeep near the cut-off and cautiously worked their way down the packed dirt road to the high fence that surrounded Lamantia's junk-yard. The gates to the yard were locked.

There was a large hand-painted sign hanging on the inside of the fence. Lamantia's Gun Shop and Surplus Warehouse Closed Today, it announced. There was a boldly painted warning at the bottom of the notice. Keep Out. Large Dogs and Guards Protect Property.

They were surprised that there were no guards visible. Only row after row of surplus equipment, and the high mesh wire fence that prevented vandals from breaking in and stealing the merchandise.

And the dog.

"A rottweiler," Lyons said in a quiet voice as he saw the massive black beast loping toward the section of fence near them. "Damn good police dogs. A few of them have saved my life over the years."

He looked back at his sidekick. Gadgets was dragging his right leg, wincing with every step he took. Ironman was aware that there was no way he could convince him to wait in the vehicle. He wouldn't have done so either had the situation been reversed.

They kept waiting for the dog to start barking. He didn't want to have to kill the animal, but he knew he would have to if it alerted the men inside to their presence.

Two men came out of a wide door, complaining to each other in low voices. Both of them were wearing faded T-shirts and jeans. And each carried a 9 mm TEC-9 slung across his arms. One of them also carried a length of chain and a paper-wrapped bundle.

"Guards or terrorists?" Gadgets asked in a low voice as they watched them scan the area from the cover of a clump of bushes.

One of the men raised his voice. "I don't give a shit what Richie says. I'm not risking my neck for a bunch of Arabs."

The other man looked annoyed. "Keep it down. We've been promised a bonus when this is all over."

The first man sounded skeptical. "Yeah, like all the other bonuses Richie's promised us. Just don't hold your breath."

"What's the difference between the two?" Ironman asked in a whisper.

The huge animal growled at the two thugs and started moving toward them. They stopped.

"Richie wants the goddamn monster inside," one of them reminded the other.

"Damn thing scares me," the other commented.

"Just throw him the meat and put the chain around his neck."

The nervous street soldier carrying the parcel unwrapped it and dropped a joint of raw meat on the ground. As the rottweiler attacked it ferociously, the man quickly wrapped the thick steel leash he carried around its neck.

The two waited until the massive canine finished eating, then together dragged him into the warehouse, walking past where Lyons and Schwarz were crouched in hiding.

Lyons looked at the Able Team science whiz. His face was cold and hard, deliberately void of any expression.

Ironman understood. All of them had suffered painful personal losses. But the commitment they had made to themselves and the others who depended on them when they joined Able Team made it impossible to allow themselves to spend more than a few moments living in the sorrow.

Without a word Schwarz picked up the AR-15 and moved closer to the fence. "Cover me," he whispered as he began to climb over the barrier.

Inside, the rottweiler began to bark loudly at the smell of the approaching intruders. Gadgets dropped to the ground and waited for Ironman to follow. Lyons climbed to the top of the fence, dropped his Galil assault rifle into Schwarz's waiting hands, then swung over the top and let himself fall. Schwarz handed the assault weapon back to him, then kneeled and pulled out the wedge-shaped carbon steel combat knife strapped to his leg.

Leading the way, he slipped behind a huge Caterpillar sitting by itself in a corner of the junk-filled yard and crouched down. Ironman copied him.

The two guards came out of the warehouse and looked around. "Richie's getting paranoid about being attacked since those foreign weirdos showed up," one of them sniggered.

"Only one who's going to be attacked is that foxy redhead," the other drooled as the two walked past where the Able Team fighters were crouching.

Gadgets exploded in anger and jumped at one of them with his combat knife, cleanly severing the jugular and carotid with one powerful sweep of the killing tool. The thug stared at him in shock for a moment, then crumbled into a heap on the ground as life pumped out of both arteries onto his combat uniform.

The second hoodlum swung his TEC-9 at Schwarz and shoved a finger in front of the trigger.

"Think again," Lyons said quietly as he quickly stood up and chopped at the man's throat with the karate-hardened edge of his palm.

He heard the small bones in the neck breaking as his palm pushed through them and ruptured the vital carotid of the guard. The once-sniggering man spun around and fell against the side of the Caterpillar, then slid slowly down into the dirt.

The team of hell-raisers stopped and listened for any sounds that might indicate their attack had been heard. There was none. Instead, the yard was filled with an eerie silence.

Despite the wound in his side, Gadgets led the way to the warehouse doors, half crouching as he ran as quickly as his injury permitted. Ironman was right behind him, moving fast to catch up when he spotted the combat uniform on the edge of the roof.

The guard was leaning over a huge unipod mounted weapon. Lyons recognized it immediately—a Barrett Model 82 light machine gun. Able Team had used it effectively themselves on previous missions.

Lyons pointed his silenced Galil at the roof and unleashed two rounds with deadly accuracy. The dead attacker fell from the edge of the roof into the junk-filled yard.

The muffled pair of explosions from the Israeli counterterrorist gun were still audible, at least to Ironman and Gadgets. They wondered if anybody else had heard them, too. The two commandos waited to see if any other attackers came out of the warehouse. But nobody did.

They peeked inside. Except for the tall stacks of surplus merchandise lined up into rows, they could see nothing in the building. It was as if the rest of the rats had run out on the three dead man outside.

Neither Ironman nor Gadgets was fooled. Attempts to lull them into similar traps had been tried unsuccessfully before. The piles of cartons were adequate hiding places for assassins. Behind any of the stacks one or more armed killers could be waiting for them to pass by.

They moved cautiously into the building, trying to make as few sounds as they could. But, even with the gum-soled shoes they were wearing, they could hear the suction sounds of their feet as they walked inside. The huge, open space exaggerated the noise of their movement, making them sound—at least to the two Able Team invaders—like a pair of elephants stomping into the warehouse.

"I wonder where they're keeping the major?" Lyons whispered to his partner.

Before Schwarz could answer they both heard the deep-throated growls of a large animal coming from behind a partially closed door near the middle of the building.

Suddenly a new piercing sound was added to it. The shriek of a woman being cruelly tortured.

"In there," Gadgets said grimly, gripping his AR-15 tightly as he turned and angrily limped toward the screaming.

He stopped short when he heard a shuffling noise from above him. Glancing up, he saw two men in combat jumpers climbing over the top of a stack from the other side. Before Schwarz could respond the men had dropped onto their stomachs and pointed their TEC-9s at the Able Team pair.

There was no time to aim. Schwarz swung his H&K-53 up and squeezed off four rounds of high-velocity M-193 ammo. The shots found their targets—the skulls of the two would-be snipers.

He didn't stop to admire his handiwork. He could hear the movement of booted feet moving toward them from the other end of the warehouse.

Someone was yelling, "The dog! Release the dog!"

Schwarz remembered the furious animal. Much tougher to deal with than the dirtbags trying to attack them. He decided to stop them before they could get the animal.

"Here's a little present for you bastards!" Gadgets shouted, reaching for the 40 mm fragmentation grenade on his belt. He pulled the pin and threw the multigrooved kill weapon in a slow, loping spin over the tops of the tall stacks.

"Nice pass," Lyons observed.

"Duck!" Gadgets yelled back as the grenade loudly exploded into thousands of deadly metal fragments across the wide room.

They could hear the wail of dying men from behind the far cartons as a small fire started inside a large cardboard section. Crouching behind packing cases, they waited to see how many men would attack. From behind them they could hear the woman scream again.

"You go ahead," Ironman said. "I'll cover for you."

Gadgets didn't stop to weigh the offer. He knew his colleague could handle ten assassins by himself. He turned and resumed his limping toward the door.

BLANCANALES PULLED UP alongside the empty jeep and parked on the side of the road. Grabbing his H&K-53 assault rifle, Pol ran to the locked gates, slung his weapon over a shoulder and quickly scaled the fence. Dropping to the ground, he cautiously moved through the junk-filled yard and found the three combat-uniformed corpses.

Gadgets and Ironman had been there. They'd left three presents behind. But where were they now? he wondered.

Suddenly the walls of the long warehouse buckled outward momentarily as a huge explosion tore through the building. The reverberations shoved Pol back a few feet.

Now, at least, he knew where they were. As he ran into the building, he wished they had less pointed ways of announcing their presence.

Ironman was standing in the middle of the room, knocking down attackers as if they were pins in a bowling alley. Blancanales rushed to his side and joined in repelling the waves of uniformed men who were shouting oaths in Arabic.

Nine men charged at them. Nine men died.

Make that eight, Lyons decided as he heard moaning from one of them. He leaned over the blood-covered, unshaven man. The man tried to speak, but the body of what had once been Richie Lamantia stopped functioning before he uttered a word.

THE ROTTWEILER TORE furiously against his chains as the sounds of gunfire and the explosion penetrated the inner room. Every moment of training he had been given by the

K-9 experts in the Kern County Sheriff's Department had returned.

His job had been to attack anyone who held a weapon—except for those in police uniforms. The memory of his training returned and started him widely straining at the thick links, trying to tear himself free.

The grenade explosion had interrupted the man on the rubber mattress. He turned away from the woman who had been the victim of his savage assault and jumped to his feet. Hollings picked up his 9 mm Glock automatic and started to walk out the door. He stopped and changed his mind.

Returning to her side, he knelt and glared into her face. "You and I aren't finished yet," he snarled. No longer was he worried about planting a top-secret document on her body. Now he just wanted her dead. Behind him he heard the furious barking of the animal Lamantia had chained to the wall. Then the screech of heavy bolts being torn from the concrete block wall.

Hollings turned as the animal leaped at him, and tried to keep the huge jaws from tearing him apart.

Somebody had entered the room. "Police dogs won't hurt you if you stay still," a new voice said.

"Get him off me," Hollings pleaded painfully as the rottweiler drew blood.

"Drop your gun first," the newcomer said.

Hollings looked at the combat-uniformed man carrying an AR-15. He hurt too much to argue. "Here it is," he said, tearing his other hand free of the growling jaws to place it on the mattress.

Two other armed men entered the room. One was dressed like the first. The other was wearing an officer's uniform.

He hurt too much to wonder who they were.

The blond man in combat fatigues leaned over and spoke softly to the black dog, calmly smoothing down the fur on the animal's back. Gently lifting the chain, he led the rottweiler out of the room.

Pol glanced at Irina's battered body and quickly turned away to hide the anger he felt. "I'd better give Ironman a hand and make sure there's nobody hiding," he said as he left.

Gadgets reached for an Army blanket and covered the major with it. "Are you okay?" he asked her. He thought about it. "I'll find another blanket," he said, turning away to look for one.

Ignoring his pain, the former KGB agent took the opportunity to edge a hand along the mattress, feeling for where he had dropped the Glock automatic.

It was gone. He turned his head slowly and looked at the redheaded woman. She held it in her tightly bound hands.

There was no mercy in her eyes. Just hate. And revenge.

Before Hollings could speak she emptied the automatic into his face. "Now I am," she said without emotion, letting the empty weapon fall from her hands.

EPILOGUE

Irina Malkova Tolstoy was sitting up in bed reading a newspaper and surrounded by flowers when Gadgets wheeled himself into her room. He smiled at the Russian major as he entered. Despite the makeup the nurses had helped her put on, he could still see the bruises and puffiness where she'd been beaten.

At least they had done something about her cruelly butchered hair. Someone had cut it into one of the short styles that were currently trendy.

She looked up and smiled back, then put down the paper.

"Anything interesting in it?" he asked.

"The rest of my team is in a place called Karnack, Texas, where they are observing the dismantling of two Pershing missiles."

"Feel left out?"

"A little," she admitted. "But I will be going home soon, so that is something."

He tried to hide his disappointment.

"What did they find when they operated?" she asked, changing the topic of conversation to one that didn't involve her imminent departure.

"Body armor never did stop armor-piercing cartridges," he said, trying to sound casual. "They said that nothing important had been seriously damaged or torn. I'll heal."

She looked relieved. "I am glad." With a sigh she added, "Perhaps when we are both better and our countries get to know each other better, we could..."

Schwarz understood. "You don't have to explain. We both have our jobs to do." He didn't bother telling her he had struck out trying to convince Brognola he should let Able Team take care of a Mexican drug kingpin named Ruiz.

They looked at each other awkwardly just as the door opened and General Cassidy, grinning happily, entered the room. He wore a sling to support his wounded arm. "You're both looking better," he commented.

"How are you, General?" Irina asked.

"Fine," he replied. Then he winked and added, "But I put in for another Purple Heart. My old mother told me never to waste an opportunity to get a medal."

The Russian major started laughing for the first time since the ambulance had delivered her to the base hospital.

"Before you continue laughing, I've got some bad news for you," the general told her.

The smile vanished from her face. Gadgets leaned forward to listen.

"You're not going home for a while," Cassidy said.

"Is something wrong, General?" she asked, looking concerned. Had her superiors found out about the evening she'd spent with Hermann Schwarz.

The general tried to keep a straight face. "I just finished talking to a Colonel Sheveresky, who claims to be your boss."

The major became tense.

Cassidy turned to Schwarz. "This involves you, too, Schwarz," he said sternly. "I had an earlier conversation with your boss, too." He stared at the two wounded warriors as he continued. "The three of us agreed that our goal for a happier relationship between our two people might be realized if the two of you were to spend two weeks as guests at MIT." He started laughing at his own joke, then stopped and looked at both of them again. "Those are orders!" he said firmly. "So I'll expect you to meet me in Cambridge when both of you get out of here."

Gadgets grinned. "Orders acknowledged," he said, then turned and looked at the Russian major.

There was a gleam in her eyes as she added, "And *spasibo*, General."

Cassidy turned to Gadgets with a puzzled look on his face. "Was she saying something nasty to me?"

"I said," Irina announced, "that I would like to give you a kiss in gratitude."

"I can remember," the general sighed as he walked to the side of her bed, "when girls wanted to kiss me for other reasons."

ABLE TEAM DICK STIVERS

Check out the action in two ABLE TEAM books you won't find in stores anywhere!

Don't miss out on these two riveting adventures of ABLE TEAM, the relentless three-man power squad:

DEATH HUNT—Able Team #50 $2.95 ☐
The lives of 20 million people are at stake as Able Team plays
hide-and-seek with a warped games master.

SKINWALKER—Able Team #51 $2.95 ☐
A legendary Alaskan werewolf has an appetite for local Eskimos
fighting a proposed offshore drilling operation.

	Total Amount	$ _____
	Plus 75¢ Postage	.75
	Payment enclosed	$ _____

More than action adventure...
books written by the men who were there

VIETNAM: GROUND ZERO™
ERIC HELM

Told through the eyes of an American Special Forces squad, an elite jungle fighting group of strike-and-hide specialists fight a dirty war half a world away from home.

These books cut close to the bone, telling it the way it really was.

> "Vietnam at Ground Zero is where this book is written. The author has been there, and he knows. I salute him and I recommend this book to my friends."
>
> —Don Pendleton
> creator of *The Executioner*

> "Helm writes in an evocative style that gives us Nam as it most likely was, without prettying up or undue bitterness."
>
> —*Cedar Rapids Gazette*

> "Eric Helm's Vietnam series embodies a literary standard of excellence. These books linger in the mind long after their reading."
>
> —*Midwest Book Review*

Available wherever paperbacks are sold.

VIE-1

by GAR WILSON

The battle-hardened five-man commando unit known as Phoenix Force continues its onslaught against the hard realities of global terrorism in an endless crusade for freedom, justice and the rights of the individual. Schooled in guerrilla warfare, equipped with the latest in lethal weapons, Phoenix Force's adventures have made them a legend in their own time. Phoenix Force is the free world's foreign legion!

"Gar Wilson is excellent! Raw action attacks the reader on every page."
—Don Pendleton

Phoenix Force titles are available wherever paperbacks are sold.

GOLD
EAGLE

PF 1R

PHOENIX FORCE

DEATHLANDS.

A different world—a different war

RED EQUINOX $3.95 ☐
Ryan Cawdor and his band of postnuclear survivors enter a
malfunctioning gateway and are transported to Moscow, where
Americans are hated with an almost religious fervor and blamed
for the destruction of the world.

DECTRA CHAIN $3.95 ☐
A gateway that is part of a rambling underwater complex brings
Ryan Cawdor and the group off the coast of what was once
Maine, where they are confronted with mutant creatures and
primitive inhabitants.

ICE & FIRE $3.95 ☐
A startling discovery changes the lives of Ryan Cawdor and his
band of postholocaust survivors when they encounter several
cryogenically preserved bodies.

Total Amount	$	_____
Plus 75¢ Postage		.75
Payment enclosed	$	_____

If you've missed any of these previous titles, please send a check or money order payable to Gold Eagle
Books.

In the U.S.

Gold Eagle Books
901 Fuhrmann Blvd
Box 1325
Buffalo, NY 14269-1325

In Canada

Gold Eagle Books
P.O. Box 609
Fort Erie, Ontario
L2A 5X3

Please Print
Name: _____
Address: _____
City: _____
State/Prov: _____
Zip/Postal Code: _____

DL-B1

"Some of the most riveting war fiction written…"
—Ed Gorman, *Cedar Rapids Gazette*

VIETNAM: GROUND ZERO.

SNIPER

ERIC HELM

The Vietnam War rages on as Special Forces Captain Mack Gerber embarks on his latest order—to assassinate top Red Chinese officials planning PLA troop protection of the Ho Chi Minh Trail.

Charlie, Gerber's nineteen-year-old hit man, is a talented sniper with twenty confirmed kills in only two months of service, but the kid has a conscience and it's got Gerber worried. Charlie's up against the best sniper in the People's Army and it only takes one shot to change things for good.